WALT DISNEY'S
ANNETTE

Mystery at
Medicine Wheel

Authorized Edition featuring ANNETTE,
star of motion pictures and television

By Barlow Meyers

Illustrated by Robert L. Jenney
and Maxine McCaffrey

WHITMAN PUBLISHING COMPANY • Racine, Wis.

Contents

1 Responsible Citizen!

Annette rose from her seat on the bus, staggered as the vehicle lurched around a curve, then sank into a seat across the aisle away from the sun.

"Whew!" she sighed. "What a trip! What a bus!"

Just for something to do, she pulled a road map out of her handbag and studied it. An hour ago her plane had landed at Greybull, Wyoming, and she had made connections with this bus which was to deposit her at the ranch of her second cousins, Sophie and Martha Lowery. They would be at the gate to meet her, Uncle

9

Archie had said when he had hung up from the long-distance call he had placed.

Had that been only yesterday? It seemed more like a year!

She looked out the window to see the gray-tan Wyoming countryside slipping past the rattling old bus. The land was shot with early June green on which occasional herds of cattle grazed. Once the bus slowed and worked its way through a band of sheep on the highway. Looking to the right, Annette could see the rolling Wyoming buttes and hills below, and she realized that the bus was actually running along the flanks of the Big Horn Mountains. Looking to the left, she saw that the hills rose higher and higher and ended in jagged mountaintops with a timber fringe not far from the top. The silver-green of aspen climbed the ravines that led upward, and rocks thrust themselves out of the mountainsides everywhere.

Usually Annette enjoyed scenery. Today she could have done without it. She wished she were back in Hollywood with Uncle Archie and Aunt Lila, wished she were sunning on the beach with the gang as she had other summers. Yet less than a week ago she had told Aunt Lila that she wished "something different would turn up" for the vacation period.

It had. Uncle Archie had turned up two cousins of whom she had heard only vaguely, and now she was on her way to their ranch to work for the summer.

She pulled out her handkerchief and mopped her

brow, noting with distaste the dust on the piece of cloth. She could not remember ever having been so warm.

She was sitting half a dozen seats behind the driver and he caught her eye as she grimaced. "Sorry about the air conditioning, miss. It would go off on the hottest day we've had so far this summer."

The air conditioning had gone off when they were less than a mile out of Greybull. The bus was a rackety affair anyhow, and its springs had given up their remaining spunk some time ago. Annette's bones ached already and there were still two hours to go.

She glanced over her shoulder at the only other occupant of the bus and turned hastily forward again. The Indian boy was staring at her, his expressionless face somehow managing to carry an animosity that showed as clearly as sun on water.

Now what did I ever do to him? she thought.

Actually, his hostility could not matter less. Annette laid her handbag against the wooden arm of the seat and leaned sideways to let her head rest on it. Although the plane trip from Hollywood to Greybull had been interesting, she was suddenly tired—of the heat, the trip, the bus, and the Indian.

"Right now I'd almost tell Uncle Archie I was sorry!" she told herself.

But it was too late for that. She let her thoughts slide back over the past two days, her eyes shut tight to keep out the view of the Indian she could see in the driver's rearview mirror.

It had been only the night before last that she had come home from the spring prom still glowing from the perfect evening. She had peeked into the den to say good night to Uncle Archie and Aunt Lila who were watching the late movie, then had made her way lightly up the stairs, feet flying in time to the waltz strains that issued from the television set. It had been an evening of magic, partly because Tom Scanlon was a very special date, and partly because her gown had been so right— really the prettiest she had ever owned. The dress had been expensive, of course, but it was perfect. She whirled a few more times in front of the full-length mirror on her closet door, enjoying the last few moments before she had to slip out of the dress and hang it away.

She sighed contentedly as she got into bed. The prom had marked the end of the school year and the beginning of summer relaxation. Plans had been laid for afternoons at the beach, tennis, golf, parties. As she fell asleep the long summer days stretched ahead invitingly, full of fun and adventure with her friends.

The next morning she had padded leisurely down the stairs, savoring again the highlights of the prom to relate to Aunt Lila over breakfast. As she approached the living room she had been startled by an angry roar from Uncle Archie. She had rushed through the doorway and found him standing in the middle of the room waving an envelope in his hand.

"Young lady, just what is the meaning of this?"

"Of what?" she had asked.

"Of this!" He had held out the envelope so that she could read the return address.

"Why, Uncle Archie, it's just the bill for my prom dress."

"*Just* the prom dress? For this amount you could have bought a whole spring wardrobe! Your Aunt Lila and I gave you permission to buy a dress, but nobody told you to spend a fortune on it!" Uncle Archie glared at her.

Aunt Lila had come in at that moment. She looked concerned, but not frantic. Usually Annette could count on Aunt Lila to take her part—that is, in a quiet way. She might suggest that Annette not protest a decision of Uncle Archie's, just wait until he simmered down. This time, however, Aunt Lila sat down and listened, her face sober as she studied Annette.

"But, Uncle Archie, it was such a beautiful dress. I just *had* to have it for the prom. I thought I could borrow on my allowance—" Annette tried to explain, but Uncle Archie seemed to have ended the conversation.

As he sat down at his desk he said coldly, "Go eat your breakfast, Annette. We'll decide what to do about this later."

As Annette ate her breakfast she noticed that the house was ominously silent. She did not want to go back to the living room and face Uncle Archie. He had ruined the memory of the previous evening by making such an issue about the dress of which she had been so proud. She just did not want to talk about it.

She went back to her room, showered, and dressed.

Then she took a deep breath and started downstairs. Maybe by now he would be cooled off and could discuss the situation calmly.

Aunt Lila was working in the kitchen. She smiled at Annette, but there was a certain quiet reserve in her greeting that made it clear that the trouble was not over yet.

Annette stood at the window for a few minutes, then turned to her aunt. "Is Uncle Archie still mad at me?"

Aunt Lila straightened, her lips making a deliberate, thoughtful O. "Yes, honey, this time I'm afraid he is."

"What else could I have done? It was the only dress I saw that was just right. I had to have it! Would it have helped if I had asked him before I bought it? I thought about that, but I was so afraid someone else would buy it if I waited to talk it over."

Again Aunt Lila was deliberate in her answer. "It might have. At least we could have discussed it. Uncle Archie might have given you permission if you had explained how important it was to you. Perhaps you could have worked out a way to earn some money to help pay the extra cost. But you know how your uncle feels about careless spending. Do just as you usually do, though, Annette. Let things rest. Perhaps he won't say more."

Annette had reflected, while she helped with the dishes, that Aunt Lila did not seem as certain of her brother's reaction as usual. Since the death of her parents in an accident several years before, Annette had made her home with her Uncle Archie and his widowed sister, Lila McLeod. Even now, riding this horrible bus on which Uncle Archie had put her, Annette was quite sure that she could not have had a better home.

She remembered Uncle Archie's almost genial tone later that morning as he had come in from his beloved garden. "Well, how are you, young lady?"

Annette had felt sudden hope that maybe Aunt Lila was right. Things were going to blow over. "I'm fine, Uncle Archie. How's the garden doing?"

He washed his hands at the sink and dried them on one of Aunt Lila's dish towels. "It's doing fine—just the way it always does in June."

There was a certain directness about him this morning. "Oh," Annette had said weakly.

Aunt Lila opened her mouth as though about to say something, then glanced at her brother and closed it again. Uncle Archie went into the living room.

"Come in here, Annette," they heard him say after a moment.

Annette and Aunt Lila exchanged glances. Annette went in and sat down on the sofa. Uncle Archie was fumbling in the drawer of his desk. The process took several minutes but finally he drew out a letter, pulled the missive from its envelope, and read it with care.

He laid it down. "Annette, I think it's high time you did something with your summers besides loaf them away on the beach with your friends."

Annette felt her mouth fall open with astonishment. For the last two summers she had wanted to get a job and Uncle Archie had discouraged the idea. "Have your childhood, Annette. There'll be plenty of time to work later."

"But—" she started.

"Let me finish," he said sternly. "About half the time lately you are overdrawing your allowance, and I've begun to realize that your knowledge of handling money is not all that it should be."

"But, Uncle Archie, if you mean the dress, the fault was mine. I should have asked—"

"But you didn't," he retorted, "and if you had I would have said no. Why a young girl like you feels it necessary to spend all that money on one dress is more than I'll ever understand. Anyway, what I have decided is to send you to cousins of Lila's and mine for a summer visit—up on a ranch in Wyoming."

"But I thought you just said I should work—"

"Exactly. This is not *just* a visit. A month ago I had a letter from Martha and Sophie saying they were going to take in some paying customers to help out on expenses this summer. That means they'll need extra help in the house—meals and so forth, you know—and I thought—"

"That I could go up and play waitress?" Annette asked. She realized she had sounded flip, and she shut her mouth firmly.

"If you want to put it so, yes. You'll learn what it

is to *earn* the money you spend, and you couldn't be among nicer people."

"How do you know that, Archie?" Aunt Lila had entered the room and lowered herself into a chair.

"Because I visited there eight years ago, when our uncle was still living. It's a beautiful place and they are our kinfolk. Also she says—Sophie, I mean—in this letter that they will take only well-recommended people for the summer."

"Recommended by whom?" Aunt Lila asked placidly.

Uncle Archie slapped his hand hard on the desk and leaned back in his swivel chair until the casters squealed with the strain. "Lila, sometimes you can obscure the issues until a person could tear his hair!"

"What are the issues?"

Her uncle raised a finger for each issue that came. "For Annette, a sense of responsibility, experience with the value of money—all done under the roof of relatives of ours so that she will be safe while she's doing it. Annette must learn to become a responsible citizen."

Annette saw an amused glint in her aunt's eye. Let Uncle Archie be provoked with his niece and he always resorted to the expression "a responsible citizen."

When she had control again, Aunt Lila asked a question. "Just how do our cousins know they're going to get any paying guests? Such ranches are usually resort places, you know. Does their ranch offer much? Do they really need the money?"

"I don't know the answer to either except that Cousin

Sophie says they already have reservations from a man and his two sons for this summer and they have built a guesthouse in the yard for them. The sisters were left with this ranch when Uncle Dan died, but they seem to think there's a chance to make more out of it than they have been."

Uncle Archie rose. He went to the closet and took out his hat.

"Archie, where are you going?" his sister asked.

"To make flight connections to the Circle Y."

Annette jerked upright. "You mean I can't drive up in my car?"

"You cannot. It will stay here for the summer."

"But why not? I've driven on other trips—long ones, too."

He turned in the doorway and looked back at her. "Because you will be there for a purpose—to learn to become a—"

"Responsible citizen." Annette said it dully. Aunt Lila said it under her breath, but they both said it. Uncle Archie's lips tightened and he went out, banging the screen door sharply behind him.

The tears came then in spite of herself. "Aunt Lila, I think he's mean!"

Aunt Lila pulled Annette against her. "No, he isn't, honey. Your Uncle Archie's an old dear, even if we did laugh at him a little. He just wants what's best for you."

Annette pulled away. "You mean you think it's best for me to have to work up there in that wilderness?

Why couldn't I wait on tables here in Hollywood? How will Wyoming make me a responsible citizen?"

"Sit down, Annette," Aunt Lila told her, smiling. "You and I have usually laughed together when Uncle Archie gets one of his brainstorms, but I'm afraid this time I agree with him. You should be learning about money, learning to work. It's not easy to get a job in Hollywood because would-be actresses have them all. At the Circle Y you can grow and develop, away from your crowd here. You'll make new friends, learn new ways, and get acquainted with your relatives."

"Be a responsible citizen," Annette said dryly.

Aunt Lila's lips twitched. "I'm a little tired of that expression so let's not use it. Anyway, enough preaching. Wash your face and gather up your laundry."

Uncle Archie arrived home two hours later. He handed Annette a plane ticket and a slip of paper with the hours of departure and arrival from Hollywood to Greybull, Wyoming. "You'll take a bus from there for about four hours. It will let you off at the ranch gate on a country road, and Sophie says she'll meet you there. They're mighty glad you're coming. You'll leave at nine tomorrow morning."

The bus slowed momentarily to ease over a large bump in the road. Even so, the jounce knocked the leather handbag out of place and Annette struck her head sharply on the wooden arm. She sat up, rubbing her head, and the driver grinned apologetically. "Not much we can do about Wyoming country roads. Every day I make this run, I just hope we make it in."

At that, the bus coughed, jerked spasmodically, gave up and died. Wearily the driver opened the door and lifted the hood.

"You may as well get out and stretch," he called back to them. "This will take a few minutes."

Annette rose and stepped outside, and the Indian boy followed a few minutes later. He said nothing to either of them, but Annette had a feeling that he was very conscious of both the driver and herself. He walked up and down slowly, but there was a tension to his lean frame, an awareness of them in his dead-pan face. He kept his face turned away from them and only his eyes seemed alive, turning this way and that to watch the country.

Annette stood at the edge of the road, looking down several miles at the Wyoming foothills. There was a haze in the air, and the sight reminded her of looking down through clear blue water to the bottom of a lake. She would have thought it beautiful if she had not been forced to come here.

"I think I can get us to a garage about ten miles ahead," the driver told them. He gestured both of them back into the bus and slid into the driver's seat, dropping a heavy wrench on the floor beside him.

An hour later, an hour of spasmodic jerking and sluggish progress, he drove off the road and up to the open door of a garage with gasoline pumps in front. A well-greased fat man crawled from beneath a car and came toward them, and for several minutes they stood looking at the motor and discussing the situation.

"You may as well get some exercise," the driver told them. "This will take an hour. You folks could call your families if you wanted to. It's only about twenty miles from here."

Annette shook her head. "I'll just wait."

She got out and walked up and down in the shade of the garage for a time. "That Indian must live somewhere close to the Circle Y," she thought. She glanced around to see that he had gotten a drink from a pump in the yard and was now climbing back into the bus. She decided to stay where she was. It was cooler in the shade.

2 A Terrifying Side Trip

If a person stayed in the shade, he had three choices: to walk a few yards back and forth in front of the garage, drink a bottle of pop from the cooler inside, or sit on the bench outside. By the time Annette had done all three for more than half an hour, she was looking for further activity.

When she saw that the driver and the garage mechanic were still bent over the motor, she walked around the corner of the garage to explore, and a few yards away from the main building, she saw a small rather shabby dwelling. Its door was closed; no one seemed to be inside or outside. There was no evident yard, for the house simply sat in the midst of a large sage area with almost buried concrete blocks creating a stepping-stone walk from garage to house. If the mechanic had a family, they did not live here.

Annette followed the walk almost to the door, then moved to the right around the dwelling, her head down to avoid snagging her hose on the coarse sage branches as she stepped around them. Still looking down as she rounded the back corner of the house, she suddenly heard a hoarse startled gasp ahead of her.

She jumped back with alarm. A young man faced her, his face startled and angry, his body half crouched as though either to flee or spring like an animal.

"Oh, I—I'm sorry!" she exclaimed. Something in the youth's face was completely frightening, and she stepped back hastily. His face was crimson with sunburn, a bad sunburn extending down to the neckline of a dirty white jersey that was much too big for him. Worst of all, his jaw was shot forward and sideways, the teeth showing like those of a creature at bay.

"I didn't mean to frighten you," she found herself saying lamely.

He straightened then, relaxing visibly, his mouth closing. He glanced around, then leaned over to pull a piece of half-rotten board out of the earth and toss it over against the foundation of the house. "It's quite all right. I—I was just cleaning up around here."

Although still too startled for clear thinking, it came to Annette, as she turned around and left, that there was little to clean up, nothing in fact but that piece of board. Hastily she made her way back to the bench in front of the garage, sat down for a moment to find herself foolishly shaken.

"What's wrong with me?" she asked in irritation. "I scared him—that was all. Everything I do is wrong lately, but I don't need to sit and shake about it."

She was shaking, nevertheless, and to forget the incident, she walked up and down again briefly until she saw the bus driver and the mechanic put down the hood of the bus.

"I'll get another battery for you to take along if you need it to finish the run," the mechanic said. The two men left the motor running as both went to the garage.

Annette entered the open door of the bus, passed the Indian boy on her way to a seat, noting that he still looked straight ahead as though unaware of her presence. It was hot inside the vehicle and she leaned her head against the window jamb and closed her eyes against the glare from outside, conscious of the throb of the motor, the slight shaking of the bus.

Suddenly she heard a quick step, opened her eyes in time to see the same sunburned youth she had seen behind the house step in, pull the lever that closed the door, throw the bus into gear, and drive wildly out onto the road with a jerk that threw Annette against the back of her seat.

For a moment she was too astonished to do more than sit and watch him, aware of the lurching and bouncing of the bus, of increasing speed, of the youth's set red face in the rearview mirror as he alternately watched his course and glanced up to see what was going on back at the garage. Behind her she heard shouts and looked back to see the two men left at the garage come running out, but she could see that only through a high rolling cloud of dust.

She turned back and pushed herself to her feet just as the Indian boy did the same thing. "Where—where are you going? What's happening?" she cried.

The Indian was starting down the aisle, and Annette saw the eyes in the mirror narrow to slits, saw the youth's lips draw back almost in a snarl as his hand dropped to the floor and lifted the big wrench the driver had left there earlier. He hefted it lightly in his hand, his blazing narrowed blue eyes resting on the approaching youth. The Indian stopped in the aisle and for a long moment, as Annette sank back into her seat, the two were locked in that exchange of looks. Slowly the Indian boy stepped back and sat down in his seat, his face only a little more rigid in its expression than it had been before.

"That's better!" the driver commented between tight lips. "But get back, kid, clear to the back of this bus. Miss, you stay right where you are. No talking."

Quietly the Indian did as he was told and when he was seated the driver laid the wrench back on the floor. In the mirror his expression changed. The blue eyes opened wide and he smiled—a bland, teasing, almost innocent look.

"But where are you taking us?" Annette cried. "What's happening?" She half rose to her feet.

"That's none of your affair," he told her firmly, the cracked sunburned lips barely moving. "Keep quiet and you won't be hurt. Sit down, I said!" He reached down for the wrench again.

Annette dropped back into her seat. He would be perfectly willing to use that wrench and it would not matter to him if he used it on man or woman. The truth of that lay in his venomous expression.

For a time then the bus went careening on down the road dipping into vales between hills, shooting around corners. Once he almost went over into a ditch, righted the vehicle and raced on.

Recovering from her first fright, Annette found her mind racing. She realized that the first thing the police would want to have was a description of their quarry. He was as yet far from quarry, but she would rather sit and think instead of merely sitting being scared. He was perhaps five feet ten in height, his hair was blond, and probably under the sunburn his skin was fair, too. His build was hard to judge beneath the too large jersey and worn cotton pants, but she guessed that he would be slender. Between her fright and the plunging bus, her head seemed to be wheeling. She forced it to work. Something unusual, something different about him—that was what the police would want to know.

Hands gripping her handbag until her fingers hurt, she hunted for some identifying feature.

"Quit staring!" the driver snapped suddenly. "You want me to drive this crate off the road?"

Annette sat back jerkily, aware that she had been leaning forward, but knowing also that when he had lifted his head to stare back at her in the rearview mirror she had seen the something unusual: the line of a scar at the point where neck and chest met. There had been some operation that left a scar.

Suddenly he braked the bus, making the wheels swivel on the graveled road. For a moment they seemed to be in a cloud of yellow dust. When it cleared she was aware that he had slowed to ordinary road speed, and she saw him reach hastily to the dash and set on his head the chauffeur's visored cap the usual driver had left there. It was too large and he set it at a jaunty angle, perched to the left as though to shade his eyes from the sun.

Suddenly Annette saw what had caused the action. Coming across the sagebrush country on a road that would cross the road they were traveling was a car— coming at a fast clip, considering the terrain. Even at a half-mile distance she could see it bouncing over sage humps and small gullies.

Annette glanced over her shoulder at the Indian boy and saw that he, too, had seen the approaching car. The driver put an end to any hopes they might have had. "Don't try it!" he warned. He dropped a hand to his trousers' pocket where there was a bulge. For the first time Annette thought about a gun. Until now, she had noticed only the big wrench. "If they come at me, somebody gets it. Don't lift a hand or yell. It may as well be you as anybody. I mean that!"

Annette had no doubt of that. She looked out the window, then found her gaze pulled back to the approaching car. She smothered a gasp. The vehicle was less than sixty yards from the crossroad now. Inside were four men, and she saw sun glinting on a rifle barrel thrust out the window. On the side of the car was STATE POLICE—WYOMING.

The driver picked up a little speed and passed the car before it reached the crossroad. He lifted his hand in a careless salute as he passed. Annette looked back. The car had pulled up on the shoulder of the road and was sitting there with two of the men looking out through the rear window at the disappearing bus. Even as she watched, it moved ahead over the hill and disappeared.

She did not know whether to feel disappointed or relieved. The situation left a horrible uncertainty about the future—or whether there would even be a future. If the police had followed them, somebody probably would have been killed. She looked at the Indian again. The boy was sitting calmly, eyes straight ahead, his hands lying palm up on his thighs. She glanced down at her own tightly gripped fists and felt a little ashamed of her fear. She forced her hands over and opened her fingers so that they lay like his.

Forcing out the tension helped her think, and she had

an unexpected thought. This man knew this road, or he could not have driven a bus over such tortuous twists and turns at such high speed.

Even as she watched, he slowed suddenly, took a narrow side road that led straight up toward the mountains on the north. She wondered what would happen if he met another car, for the space was too narrow for passing, the roadside was lined with rocks and gullies. The bus bounced and jolted. Once she turned to see the Indian flung half out of his seat. She had to cling to the seat in front of her to keep from being bruised against the sides.

Through the next half hour she was conscious that the bus was climbing steeply. The driver often threw it into low gear, and the narrow road twisted and turned steadily, following the edge of a canyon. Only a short way ahead she could see the timberline, which only a few hours ago had looked ten miles up from the roadway. Looking down, she could see the narrow line of roadway they had left. It was despairingly far away.

Suddenly the bus slowed. The roadsides had opened out on each side into open parks just below the timberline. The driver swung the wheel and ran the bus down a long slope. It was in a tilted position following the line of the mountain and Annette feared it would go over. Then he eased the bus down a rocky slope and pulled under a small stand of spruce trees.

So jolted she was shaky, but so numb with apprehension she could hardly move, she watched him brake the bus, cut the motor and turn around. Deliberately he surveyed the two of them, a sardonic amusement in his examination. He flexed his shoulders as though they were tired, pulled the lever that opened the door, and picked up the big wrench.

"Get out."

He went out ahead of them and stood a few feet away from the door waiting, wrench ready in his hand. Slowly Annette got to her feet and moved stiffly down the aisle with the Indian coming along behind her. She had a horrible wonderment about what the man with the wrench was going to do.

Once they were on the ground, he stepped back and gestured west. "Start walking."

They had hardly started when he stopped them. "Hold it! I want whatever money you've got."

Reluctantly Annette opened her handbag for her billfold. She drew from it the ten dollar bill that was all she had. He snatched it from her hand and turned toward the Indian. The boy shook his head, spread his hands beside his pockets.

"I said cough it up!" the driver snapped.

Slowly the brown hand slid into the right pocket, came out with a single half dollar. "That's all I got."

For a moment Annette thought the driver would attack the youth, there was such murderous fury in his face. He took the coin, gave the boy a shove that almost flung him against the fender of the bus. "Start walking."

The strap of her handbag was pulling on her wrist

and as she passed the door of the bus, she tossed the bag inside. It could do her no good now.

"Get that!" the driver ordered. "No leaving evidence around."

What would he call evidence? There were suitcases inside behind the seats—two of them. There was the bus itself. It was strange how one's mind worked at a time like this. She regretted that ten dollars. Only hours ago she had resented Uncle Archie's forcing her to learn something about money. Now she had lost the basis on which she was going to prove she could build finances. Suddenly she could have wept with fury.

The Indian had righted himself and was starting to walk away in the indicated direction. Annette fell in beside him, and the driver stopped her. "Walk behind him."

Wrench in one hand, the other close to the pocket with the bulge, he came along behind them, occasionally telling them where to go. For a time they followed the bank of a roaring mountain stream, and finally he told them to turn left up a ravine. The climb was difficult and rough. In her flat shoes she had a hard time keeping up with the boy ahead of her, and behind her the driver was always too close for comfort.

She was also aware that the sun was getting over to the west, hidden behind the top of the mountain they were climbing. The air here was cold although she herself was perspiring with the speed and difficulty of the climb.

Then abruptly the ravine ran out, ending in a narrow rocky area filled with small boulders. "Stop here!" the driver ordered.

Annette stepped up, panting, beside the Indian and turned. Her throat seemed to be constricting with fear until she could hardly breathe. The driver was perhaps six feet below them, still climbing, his gaze on them. Beside her, the Indian was breathing easily, lightly, and she felt a waiting in him, a full consciousness of what could happen now.

A rock rolled beneath the driver's foot, momentarily throwing him off balance just before he reached the top. In that second of advantage the Indian flung himself forward and down like a diver off the end of a springboard. He struck the man below, a fireball of desperate determination. The driver saw him coming, but he had no time to raise his wrench high enough to strike. The two collided—went over and back. Annette heard the driver's head strike on a rock, heard his single moan.

Then the Indian slowly rose from on top of his victim. He stayed bent over a minute, one hand on the driver's chest as though to hold him down, the other reaching for the pocket with the bulge. He straightened then, holding in his hand a rock the size of a small revolver. He flung it aside with a sound of annoyance, picked up the dropped wrench and flung it out and far down the mountainside.

Annette broke her paralysis and moved to the edge of the ravine. "Is—is he dead?"

He glanced up at her. "I dunno. Maybe. I think his head hit on the rock. Let's get out of here before he comes to. It's our only chance."

She jumped down off the ledge and moved behind him as he started down. "But—shouldn't we do something with him? Tie him up, maybe, so the authorities . . . ?"

He glanced over his shoulder at her with a faint wry humor breaking his impassive face. "How? Tie him up with what? I was just lucky tackling him like that. He's bigger'n me. Bigger'n you, too. Let's get out of here before he comes to."

He didn't wait for her to agree or disagree. For Annette it was follow or be left alone. She hurried after him, and became aware that at the bottom of the ravine he turned right and climbed diagonally along the side of the mountain upward to another round-topped hill.

"Where—where are you going?" she gasped. It was hard to keep up with him, for his long legs covered more ground than hers possibly could.

"Past the Wheel."

"Wh-what's the Wheel?"

He did not answer, and a few minutes later he came out on top of the round-topped mountain. Here the wind hit with surprising strength and the cold cut through her cotton blouse. She glanced behind her, then touched the Indian's arm and pointed below.

He stared where her finger pointed, then his face broke in the first real trace of expression she had yet seen. From here they could see into the ravine they had left, and there the man, half a mile away, was just pushing to a sitting position. He sank back, his hands to his head.

"His head will hurt for a while," the Indian said quietly.

"Let's get out of here!" Annette cried. "He'll try to run us down."

"Not now," he replied quietly. "He can't hurt us now."

"How do you know he can't?"

"This is the Indian Medicine Wheel. He can't touch us here."

He had made a sweeping gesture with his hand and Annette pulled her eyes away from the ravine and looked around. The whole round top of the mountain was covered with stones, and vaguely she saw that they were arranged in a design, an oval wheel with spokes. Inside the main ring were several piles of the gray-white stones, shaped in a scattered way, almost like seats facing east.

"What—what is it?" Annette asked.

He did not answer, did not even seem to hear. His face was turned up toward the east, his hands and arms spread out and lifted slightly. She looked again at the area and saw that this was nothing of recent building, that whatever this was, it had been constructed long ago.

She shivered, hardly knowing whether it was the cold

wind or the area that made her do so. The Indian boy's lips were moving and his eyes were closed.

Almost suddenly, he dropped his arms and moved away. "He can't get us now. Come on."

"How do you know he can't?"

"Because I've prayed at the Medicine Wheel."

3   *Indian Guide*

Without further explanation he left the spot with long rapid strides that made Annette trot to keep up with him. So far as the Indian was concerned, she might not even have been present, for he neither paused nor looked back until they had traversed a long gentle slope across the top of the mountain to the east and entered the fringe of timber below the bald crown. There, screened by cedars, he paused and looked past her, his eyes squinting to probe the hollows that might conceal a pursuer.

"What do you think he'll do? Who do you think he is?" Annette asked.

He shook his head. "He won't waste time on us. I don't know who he is unless—"

His gaze went past her. He seemed briefly thoughtful. Soon, he walked on, leaving her to follow as best she could.

She pattered after him, struggling to keep up, but determined to discuss this experience the two of them had shared. "But why take the two of us to the top of a mountain on a bus—of all things?"

His indifferent shrug was barely perceptible as he strode. "He probably was pushed from behind. Remember the car with the police? He grabbed the first thing to get away. Nobody in his right mind would wear clothes four sizes too big for him unless he'd stolen them. I'll bet there's a prison uniform hidden somewhere in the sage."

"Do you think he planned to kill us?"

For the first time in the six hours she had been in his presence he turned and gave her deliberate attention. The scrutiny, however, was no compliment. Annette could not remember facing a look of such scorn and dislike. "Of course he planned to kill us! Even you knew that! We were the only witnesses who had seen him close enough to be able to identify him. He had to kill us."

He turned and strode on so fast that his intent seemed to be to leave her as far behind as possible. Although squelched, Annette was angered. *I'll keep up with him if it's the last thing I ever do!*

As he traveled ahead of her, she took in details about him. The boy was tall for his age, and his copper-brown body was dressed in a blue work-shirt and cotton trousers. His tennis-shod feet put themselves down in the rubble of loose rock on the trail with a soft quick precision that amazed Annette, whose flats were slipping and sliding in every direction. He had not had a haircut for some time, for his straight black hair hung almost to the collar of his shirt.

Suddenly he turned off the trail and cut straight down the side of the mountain.

"Where are you going?" Annette gasped despite her determination to ask him nothing.

"Back to the service station. We'll have to report."

"But why don't we take the bus back? Can't you drive?"

He gave her again that look of withering scorn. "You didn't notice, I suppose, that the bus was about to run out of gas. It wouldn't have gone another mile."

"But my suitcases are there!" Annette exclaimed.

His lips twitched sardonically. "You want your suitcases! You want to be dead, too? He's probably at that bus waiting for us. I probably wouldn't be so lucky if I tackled him again as I was before."

Within minutes Annette was completely lost, and within the next hour she was aware that getting safely out of these mountains depended on her ability to stay at the Indian's heels. He traveled, almost without pause, down through brief stretches of timber, carefully skirting any open parks to avoid being sighted from above. He crossed areas of rock and rubble, climbed around or over long stretches of snowbank on which Annette's flat shoes slipped even more than on the rocks. She fell a dozen times and she fell farther and farther behind. When she had left Hollywood, her shoes had been new and had fit closely. Now they were like a pair of old bedroom slippers, loose and floppy, and she kept them on her feet only by remembering that she could not walk barefoot on rocks without them.

For two hours she managed to keep the pace. Then she found herself falling still farther and farther behind. He neither stopped nor looked back.

The day was drawing to a close, the sun far west beyond the top of the mountain of the Medicine Wheel. Although she was wet with perspiration, she could feel the wind cutting through her blouse. They were still very high, and she wondered what the Indian would do when dark came. She knew with despair that she would never be able to travel through the dark in the flat shoes.

"I'll never wear flats again as long as I live!" she promised herself. "If I live."

One shoe came off suddenly, flew through the air and struck the Indian boy on the heel. He glanced down behind him, saw the shoe, picked it up and tossed it back at her without a word. Before he faced front again, she saw something in his face that braced her failing determination. There had been amusement and mockery in his black eyes.

She could have wept with rage. *Why?* she asked herself as she put the shoe back on a foot from which bushes and rocks had almost torn her hose. Nothing but shreds remained. Her feet were bruised and sore, dusty and stained. *What have I ever done to him?*

Her determination back, she managed in the next fifteen minutes to close the gap that had steadily widened between them. A deep twilight was covering the mountain when suddenly he pulled up in front of her so suddenly that she crashed into him. He thrust out a brown arm so that she could grab it and right herself. Gasping for breath, she stared up at him.

"What's wrong with you?" she cried.

Suddenly he laughed aloud, glancing up and down at her before he turned indifferently away. Her skirt had ripped when they had come through a blackberry tangle farther back, and her blouse had one sleeve half ripped out around the armhole. He laughed aloud again but before she could utter the angry words that rose to her lips, he turned away.

"We'll have to stop for the night. You'll never make it in," he told her dryly.

"Don't let me stop you!" she retorted. "Just go on by yourself."

He let out a brief grunt, but the scorn and amusement faded out and were briefly replaced by something else. She was uncertain of its meaning, but when he glanced around him and up at the sky, she divined that he doubted if he could have traveled at night himself in this country.

With his usual abruptness he turned suddenly and dropped with catlike springiness into the six-foot depths of a ravine before which they had stopped. The ravine began where water had washed the earth from the foot of a rock ledge, leaving a bare flat floor of rock for a few yards before it plunged on down the mountainside.

After a moment of looking about, he glanced up at her, noting that she was shivering now in the cold wind. "Get down here," he remarked, an order rather than an invitation.

Because he moved down the ravine, picking up sticks and handfuls of pine needles, she turned away and began picking up sticks herself. He did not notice. As she returned to the edge of the gully a few minutes later with an armload of sticks, he was on his knees in the center of the area pushing the needles and the sticks into a small pile. She flung the sticks at his feet with a crash that was intentional and even from a kneeling position he jumped a yard away, landing crouched and tense, staring up at her with his black eyes startled and angry.

With all the strength she had left, Annette gave him a smile as loaded with mockery as she could make it. "Scared?"

She turned away indifferently and began picking up larger sticks then because, having been a Girl Scout, she knew these would be the next thing needed. Regardless of what this Indian thought, she could build a fire.

Minutes later, dark had closed down too closely even to see another stick. As Annette slid down into the ravine, wincing when her weight came onto her sore feet, he was bent over the small pile, opening a match pack. He paused in an almost controlled dismay as he saw there were only two matches left in it.

He glanced up at her and for the first time in their brief and hectic acquaintance made a voluntary statement. "Well, with luck—maybe—"

Annette could not resist a temptation. "Maybe you should have prayed at the Medicine Wheel for luck."

She was immediately sorry, for he sat back on his heels and looked at her tight-lipped and angry. Then he looked down at the match pack and replied quietly, "It could be."

As he bent forward cupping the match pack in the palm of his hand while he readied one match to strike, Annette held her breath. The match flared just as a small puff of wind blew down over the edge of the ravine. It promptly went out. Annette's breath let out in a disappointed sigh.

This time the Indian put his hands in almost under the pile of twigs, grass, and needles. When the last match flared he held it so close that Annette saw the pile catch almost immediately, the flames leaping up and through the tangle. The boy stayed kneeling beside it until he was sure, then rose and gestured Annette toward the space between the fire and the wall. As she sank down, slipped off her shoes and extended her tired feet toward the warmth of the blaze, she realized he had chosen a spot for the night where the fire would warm the wall as though it were a room. Already the fire was reflecting heat. She sighed with utter weariness.

He came around and sat down about eight feet away. "There's wood enough to last the night—if I'm careful," he said quietly. "In the morning we'll start early. I have to get to work."

"Where do you work?"

"Circle Y. I work there summers when I'm not in school."

As he heard her surprised breath, he glanced at her sullenly. "What's wrong with that? I suppose you never worked a day in your life!"

She started to snap back a retort, then thought better of it. An answer could wait. She was spending the summer working at the Circle Y, too. She hoped she was around to see his expression when he found that out!

"What's your name?" she asked him.

He opened his eyes long enough to answer. "John Running." He pulled up his knees and laid his head against them. Annette sensed that he was almost instantly asleep.

Annette had seen Indians only at a distance, and in the few waking minutes in which she let the warmth penetrate her body to the point of sleepiness, she wondered why he disliked her so.

"I don't know how an Indian really feels about anything," she reminded herself. "Maybe he thinks because
I'm a girl I can't take this kind of punishment, and he's
taking the chance to rub it in."

As the fire warmed and relaxed her and she felt sleep
coming in spite of the hard rock under and behind her,
she had a last waking thought. *Tomorrow he won't
hear a yelp out of me if I tumble headlong off a cliff!*

During the night she was aware that occasionally
John Running tended the fire and that only toward
daylight did they run out of fuel and the cold roused
her painfully but fully. As she sat up he was standing
in the gray light a dozen yards down the ravine staring
out and down the way they had to go.

He turned suddenly and almost shouted at her. "Let's
get started!"

She jumped. "What are you yelling about?"

He looked at her in surprise as she climbed to her
feet, rubbing the cold and the ache out of her arms and
shoulders. She could have moaned at the soreness of her
limbs. As she thrust her feet into her shoes, she knew
immediately that her feet were not only stiff but swollen.
She managed to keep from showing how she felt, and
though every step was agony she walked toward him.
"I'm ready."

It was the last thing she said to him for the next six
hours, or he to her. Although she had to bite her tongue
repeatedly to accomplish last night's decision, she refused to ask a question or plead for a letup in the pace

he set. By midmorning she could feel the holes in the soles of her flats, and some of the puffed places on her feet were scraped raw. If he glanced back—which he did only twice that morning—she made herself walk without limping. To give herself leeway, however, she dropped behind him perhaps a hundred feet, which permitted her to give vent to her feelings whenever he rounded a bend ahead of her and was out of sight.

By noon the air was hot and windy, but far in the distance she could see the faint line of a road with a car crawling along it, and finally she could make out the dot that must be the garage they had left so precipitously yesterday. Finally, he walked ahead of her out into flat sage country. She blinked when suddenly he disappeared entirely.

She found him kneeling at a spring beside a rock. Without so much as glancing at her he wiped his mouth on his shirt sleeve and strode away. She could not hold back a sob of sheer pain and weariness as she dropped beside the spring. There had been water flowing down from the snowcaps most of the way down, but not for the past few hours. She drank deeply, then lay flat beside the spring, bathed her face, flung the water over her hair and shoulders.

She made no attempt to catch up with him when she went on. He was almost a half mile ahead, but by now she could see the garage buildings less than two miles away and she took her time, letting herself relax. She saw him reach the building, and a moment later two men came out and stared across the sage toward her, then one came walking in her direction. In her relief at seeing a human face other than the Indian boy's, she hurried, caught her toe on a sage branch and fell head-long. She was just sitting up as the man reached her.

"Here, child! You're about all in! Let me help."

He lifted her to her feet and helped her walk along. It took an incredibly long time to reach the garage, and when she sank into a swivel chair in the shade of the office, Annette had a moment when she thought she was going to faint. She saw then that the man who had met her was in uniform. He brought her a glass of water and smiled down at her.

"There are ranchers, police, everybody, out hunting you two. Rest a minute. Then tell us what happened. The police found the bus up on Medicine Mountain early this morning, but they've been frantic over what happened to you two. This Indian kid's been in trouble before, but he's never gone in for kidnapping. This time he's really going to catch it."

Annette's mind was still hazy, and she tried to concentrate. The outline of the officer was wavering a little in her sight, but outside she could hear a loud voice asking questions, hear the husky voice of the Indian denying accusations.

"I didn't drive that bus away! I was a passenger on it, just like that girl was. I was going to my job—down at the Circle Y!"

Annette's thinking cleared. She tried to get to her

feet. "Wh-what do you mean—the Indian running away with the bus? He didn't drive it! That—that other man—the sunburned one—he was the one who drove it off—with us in it."

Suddenly everything went black and she could only feel herself falling forward.

When she came to she was lying on top of a desk. Someone was washing her face with cold water, which felt heavenly. "She's coming 'round," a man's voice said.

Annette opened her eyes. "He didn't do it."

"Easy now," the voice said again. "Time to talk later. George, go call the Lowery sisters. Tell 'em we've found their cousin."

Fifteen minutes later Annette told the story in full, with the officer taking notes, the garageman listening, and with John Running, sitting sober-faced biting his lip.

"Miss, could you give us a description of whoever it was that drove you off?"

Annette gave it to him, and the officer and the garageman exchanged a look. "John, I guess that lets you off the hook," the officer said quietly. "Lucky for you, too! The man you—the man who ran off with you probably is the convict that escaped the Rawlins penitentiary last week." He turned to the garage owner. "George, what made you so sure it was John Running who swiped that bus?"

George turned a dull red. "Well, why not? We couldn't see for the dust. He'd been in trouble before. It—well, it seemed natural."

The officer, frowning over his notes, turned back to Annette. "Miss, you're sure of the facts you've told me?"

Annette nodded weakly. "I certainly am! If it hadn't been for John here, I never would have made it. I didn't know where I was—or—or anything."

She found herself suddenly wanting to giggle at her own reversal of feeling about this Indian. "An hour ago I'd have liked to scalp him!" she thought. "Now here I am defending him."

The officer glanced at her torn clothes, frowning still. "He evidently didn't make it very easy on you," he remarked coldly.

Annette managed a grin. "That's all right. I got here." She glanced at John Running's sullen face. "What have you got against him anyhow?"

The officer shrugged. "He's been in minor trouble, doesn't like whites—that is, except the Lowery sisters. I'm surprised he didn't just go off and leave you up there."

Annette did not tell him how close she had been to being left behind most of the time. "My suitcases—were they still on the bus?"

The officer jerked his head toward the corner where her dusty suitcases were sitting. "All there—and your handbag. John, you owe this lady thanks for getting you out of a jam. I hope you appreciate it."

John said nothing. Finally words burst from him a moment later. "Me! You always blame me!"

"You ask for it," he was told. "Come on, men, and

get out of here so the lady can clean up a little. Miss Sophie's on her way down here now."

When they had gone out of the office and closed the door, Annette went wearily barefoot across the room to look at herself in the dingy mirror hung over a washbowl. Her mouth opened in shock. Her dark curly hair was matted and loaded with dust, her face dirty, red with sunburn and scratches from branches, and her clothes were gray with dirt.

She washed her face, arms, and neck, combed her hair as well as she could, threw her flats in a wastebasket and got bedroom slippers from her suitcase. They were the only things she could get on her feet.

When she walked out front, the officer and George were standing by the pumps talking. John Running saw her coming. He walked over to stand in front of her, his face showing embarrassment. Trying to be as expressionless as before, he made her an odd ducking little bow.

"I want to thank you. I did not deserve to be helped. I helped you not at all. But for you, I could now be in jail."

He turned stiffly away and separated himself by the length of the service station, where he sat on the bench looking off into the distance.

The officer went inside and telephoned a report of the finding of Annette and John Running to headquarters. He spoke to Annette when he came out. "You'll probably have to come to headquarters at

Greybull and file your account of the story," he told her, "but it can wait."

There was the sound of a motor. A jeep wheeled up to the gas pumps, and a short pudgy woman in jeans, boots, and a wide hat shoved herself to the ground and came dashing around the jeep up to Annette.

"Annette, honey, it's me. Your cousin Sophie!"

4   *Circle Y*

Annette was gathered to the pudgy figure with force and enthusiasm. Cousin Sophie's arms were powerful. She was pushed away then and a pair of keen blue eyes behind glasses looked her up and down.

"My goodness! If you aren't a sight! Never expected a relative of mine to land with herself in that shape." She whirled to the officer. "Great Scott, Grover Landis! Couldn't you do better than let that Nally boy run loose out of jail, terrorizing everybody, especially my own kinfolk?"

Officer Landis was not smiling as he replied, "We're trying, Miss Sophie, but you know that Nally case has been a tough one from the first. The report was out that he'd slipped the penitentiary, but we weren't doing more than keeping an eye out for him on regular patrol in these parts because we didn't think he'd have nerve enough to try and reach home. He outguessed us there."

Cousin Sophie's reply was dry and without humor. "He certainly did! That boy never stopped at anything. The best thing that could happen would be for his mother to stop trying to excuse him for everything and just let the authorities handle his case. John Running!" She clapped her hands down hard on his shoulders. "Boy, I'm glad to see you alive, too! How was school this last winter?"

Annette turned to see the Indian boy standing in front of Sophie, his dark face split with a shy grin that put him in a class with the rest of the human race. Annette, tired as she was, could not help being surprised at how attractive he became when he smiled.

"Let's get home!" Sophie almost shouted. "You both look tuckered. We can talk later."

She was piling Annette's baggage into the back of the jeep when Officer Landis came up and spoke quietly. "Miss Sophie, keep your doors locked. You never know."

She turned to him and nodded. "As good as done, Grover. I hope you catch him. I don't think he'll bother us though—not after this matter!"

Landis shook his head. "He might—just because of

that, Miss Sophie. Just watch it."

The only ride Annette could remember having in her life that was any more wild than the one she took to the Circle Y with Cousin Sophie was the one on the bus. She drove as though she thought Annette and John, in their spent condition, might not last until they got home. Annette clung wearily to the edge of the seat and hoped she would not be catapulted out over the Wyoming scenery every time Sophie crested the top of a hill. John Running was apparently used to the situation—or else determined not to show alarm. Once Annette looked back to see how he was taking the ride, but he was looking out over the country without apparent trepidation.

The jeep suddenly slowed, whirled off the road under an archway of poles with CIRCLE Y in short wooden lengths at the top. They sailed on across a sagebrush area toward a patch of green half a mile away.

"That's the spread," Sophie shouted over the noisy jeep with satisfaction. "My father's place. Mine and Marthy's now. We're goin' to make it pay off if it busts us wide open."

Annette was tempted to ask why it was not paying off, decided she was too tired to care, and kept silent. Sophie braked to a stop beside a brown wooden pole fence around a patch of grass, flanked with cottonwood trees. In the midst of this verdant spot a low ranch house, the bottom half of weathered logs, the top half of white clapboard, looked down a valley to the north and south, and up to the Big Horns several miles away on the west. Tired and indifferent as she felt, Annette had to admit the setting was lovely.

John had already lifted her suitcases from the back of the jeep and she followed him and Sophie up the stepping-stone walk to a wide low door in which a tall spare woman was waiting.

"Meet your Cousin Marthy," Sophie told her. Annette felt her hand taken in a grip only a little less firm than Sophie's, and she looked into an unsmiling face that swept her head to toe with an examination that missed nothing.

"Looks like you got the worst of it," Martha remarked conversationally. Her voice had a brittle quality as though not too often used—as though perhaps she rationed it to make it last.

Annette could only nod, and Martha turned back into the room. Annette could see that it was wide, low, pleasant, and obviously the main room of the house.

"Sit down," Sophie told her. "Marthy was getting ready to feed you two when I lammed out of here."

Martha was already setting filled plates at the table by the window. Annette could not decide if she was too hungry to sleep or too sleepy to eat, but she sat down and started. Halfway through, however, she laid down her fork and looked at her hovering cousins. "It's good—but I guess I'll have to sleep before I can finish."

"This-a-way then!" Sophie barked. "We got a tub

for you first. Here! Strip off and climb in."

On the floor of her small bedroom Annette saw a big washtub, a third filled with water. Martha entered carrying a steaming teakettle, poured it in, and gestured her forward. "Get in and soak. Then get to bed."

Water had never felt so good. Annette soaked her tired body, gave herself as vigorous a toweling as her sore muscles would stand, and pulled pajamas from the suitcase Sophie had left open on a chair. Martha opened the door long enough to thrust a tube of sunburn lotion through to her, and Annette annointed herself and crawled into bed. She did not even remember the bed coming up to meet her.

She awakened at midmorning of the next day and pushed up on the bed trying to think where she was. Every muscle still hurt, but not as badly as the day before. As she looked around the small plain room, she was suddenly homesick. She caught a glimpse of herself in the watery mirror atop an old dresser across the room and was suddenly annoyed with herself because she thought of Uncle Archie and that tears and a sorry-for-yourself feeling was exactly what he would have predicted. Even though he would never know, she was not about to give him that satisfaction.

She climbed out of bed and dressed. Her naturally curly hair gave her trouble, for it was matted with dust, sticky from perspiration. Her skin was already beginning to peel from the sunburn.

"I'm a sight!" she thought. "But I suppose it doesn't

matter much out here in the wilderness."

Martha turned as she appeared in the kitchen door.
"Well, you came to!" she said as though it were something she thought well overdue.

"You should have awakened me," Annette told her.
"I didn't mean to sleep all that time."

Sophie walked in at that moment, a pail in her hand.
"Well, good afternoon! How you feeling?"

She halted her short broad body solidly before
Annette and looked her over with a wide smile. "You
don't look so bad. Does she, Marthy?"

Martha approached Annette, laid her fingers on her
arm and pinched lightly. "Nope. Fine strong girl." She
turned back to the stove, picked up a cup and saucer,
and poured Annette a cup of coffee from a big granite
pot on the back of the stove. "You want breakfast or
want to wait for noon dinner?"

Annette did not want to ask special favors. "This will
do until dinner." She lifted the cup and swallowed
coffee so strong that she could only sit and stare straight
ahead of her trying to get used to it.

Sophie's lips twitched. "You'll get used to it. Ranch-
men want it stout enough to last the day, float an ax-
head, or hold up the roof in a windstorm."

Annette got her breath back and asked a question.
"When—and where shall I start work?"

She thought Martha started to speak but Sophie cut
in quickly. "Take the rest of the day off, then get
started tomorrow. We'll start you out easy. You can

look around today, get acquainted with the place."

"How is John?"

"Oh, John's fine. Thinks he had a great adventure."

"He told me he works for you every summer," Annette said.

Both the cousins nodded. Sophie explained, "John was born here on the ranch. His mother and father worked here, but his father wasn't much good and was never heard of after a time. Ruth Blue Sky stayed on with us for several years, then died of the Indian's worst ailment inherited from the white man—tuberculosis. John was eight then. We took care of him. He goes to school over on the reservation winters, but comes back here to work summers. He considers this his home."

"But why does he hate all white men the way he does?" Annette asked. "I know there were all the pioneer wrangles, but that was a long time ago."

"Not to John Running," Martha cut in in her dry rasping voice. "He's going to keep Custer's men on the run the rest of his life if he can. I'm surprised he even apologized to you, but it's a good sign since you'll be around for the summer. John probably asks for a lot of his trouble. He's not an easy youngster to handle. He's stubborn and wants his own way. If Sophie and I didn't know our own minds, he'd have a dozen arguments with us every day. We just tell him if he doesn't want to do things our way he can go back to the reservation. He's a wanderer, and sometimes he trespasses. Just because he is an Indian, that makes property owners suspicious and they report him to the police. He's never done any real harm anywhere and people would lose nothing if they just ignored him. When they complain, the police have to scold him. Then he fights with them because he doesn't want to be stopped. I understand the reservation school has had a few problems, too. Even so, John's no delinquent."

Sophie had dumped a strainer of potato peelings and kitchen leftovers in her pail, and she turned to the door. "I'll have to keep going. Want to come see the chicken house? That'll be part of your job when you start."

Annette trailed her down a path to a fenced pen about a hundred feet from the house. Sophie made a wide swing with her pail and strewed the contents in an arc. "Give them a bucketful of grain from this bin," Sophie instructed her. "Once a day, plus any kitchen stuff, and be sure the gates are shut and *locked* every night. Be on the watch for any varmint lurking around. We seem to be losing hens lately—one at a time."

"What's doing it?"

Sophie shrugged. "Dunno—yet, and haven't had the time to watch. Now that John's back, I'll set him on the trail. Could be a coyote—although they rarely come this close—or an owl."

She headed off then for other parts leaving Annette to look out for herself. Beginning with the yard, Annette circled it, pausing to glance through the open door of an obviously new neat one-room guesthouse furnished with three single beds, a dresser, easy chair, and a worktable.

The three beds were new and matched, but the rest of the furnishings were obviously taken from the house to complete the outfit. Fresh-looking tailored drapes and a waxed floor made the small house attractive.

From the yard Annette moved out toward the stable, empty at the moment, but Sophie and John were maneuvering several calves from one corral into another. Annette stepped up on the rail fence near the opening to watch. Promptly the calves bolted wildly past John Running and circled about the corral kicking up their heels and butting each other.

Because she made no connection between herself and the incident, Annette remained where she was, a little puzzled that John, starting back to reround his quarry, gave her a black look.

The calves came halfway, whiffed at her and fled again. "Get your skirt down off that fence!" John snapped at her.

"Shut up, John!" Sophie told him. "When telling's to be done, I'll do it. Honey, that cotton skirt blowing in the wind is scaring the wits out of my livestock. They aren't used to skirts. Come to the corrals in pants, like me."

Annette retreated hastily, compelled to note from a distance that the calves, once imbued with the idea of sport for any excuse whatever, gave Sophie and John a difficult fifteen minutes and that she had been the cause. When they had finally been pushed into the far corral, Annette apologized. Sophie patted her shoulder.

"Don't let John get you down, honey. Tell him off even if he's right. That's the only language we've ever been able to make him understand. About clothes around here—just don't let anything blow. Sometimes stock scares, sometimes they just use it as an excuse to scare."

She strode away, beckoning over her shoulder. "Got something to show you."

One hand clutching her full cotton skirt, bunched to one side, Annette followed her behind the stable. Sophie put two fingers to her teeth. A blasting whistle cut the Wyoming air. A quarter of a mile away Annette saw a small band of horses, bunched and grazing. They raised their heads, ears pitched toward the corrals for a moment. Then one moved forward. Not to be outdone, another suddenly started running and the next moment a stampede was headed for Annette and Sophie.

The horses gathered at the fence. "Hold down your skirt and get acquainted with the little bay mare at the end," Sophie told her. "She's your mount for the summer."

"You mean—I'll have time to ride?" Annette exclaimed in delight.

"Why, yes, from time to time," Sophie said with a carefully sober face. Annette suspected humor behind the remark, and that Sophie knew something of what had happened back in Hollywood. "That mare's gentle but she's lively. How much have you ridden?"

By now Annette was running her hand down the mare's head, blowing softly against her nose while the

animal, ears pitched forward, followed her breath up to her nostrils. It was a trick that the riding master at the stables in Hollywood had taught her to get acquainted with horses.

"I haven't ridden the way you folks do out here, I know," Annette told her. "Uncle Archie gave me a year's riding lessons for Christmas a year ago, and I went twice a week. I've probably still got lots to learn."

Somehow she had expected Sophie to scorn the English type of riding. Instead, her cousin nodded. "With that much behind you, you won't have trouble picking up Western riding. It's a matter of sitting a little deeper in the saddle, learning how to handle your weight to help the horse. If you can handle yourself and the horse, we may send you out with stock sometimes. Sam needs help when I have to keep John around the place. You can fill in the chinks."

Annette, still running her hand down the little mare's neck, was looking up toward the mountains. One great round peak made her think, with a shiver, of where she had been only yesterday. "How far to the top of that peak over there?" she pointed.

"Five miles as the crow flies, twenty miles up and down," Sophie said promptly.

"What is the Medicine Wheel?"

Sophie glanced at her. "Now where'd you ever hear of that? I didn't know anybody but the natives around here knew of it."

"It's where we got away from that convict yesterday."

"You did?" Sophie's voice was high and a little shrill. "Heaven's sake, child, you *were* up in the mountains. The Wheel—well, nobody really knows. It's been written up in magazines, and the experts say it was built by a race before the memory of man here in America. Did you see it?"

Annette nodded. "John climbed there, after he'd tackled that bus driver. He prayed there."

Sophie nodded. "That doesn't surprise me. The Indians have used it for years, and that in spite of all the mission work they learn. I didn't realize John knew where it was, but I know he and his mother, Ruth Blue Sky, used to go off on pilgrimages of their own. Maybe he knows more about it than the rest of us."

She was silent a moment, thinking about the matter, her keen blue eyes staring thoughtfully up toward Medicine Mountain.

Little as she liked to remember the events of the past two days, Annette was curious about one thing. "This Tom Nally—the one the police think escaped from prison—did he live around here?"

Sophie pointed north to a hollow of the valley. Annette could see a strip of green and a few small rooftops. "That's the Nally farm. Tom's mother and his sister live there. His father died last year. The family has never been popular, maybe on account of Tom being a ne'er-do-well, maybe just because they aren't mixers, or maybe because they have tried to protect their son from his mischief past the point where anybody should be protected. I'm guessing. So is anybody else."

"Why was he in prison?"

"Robbed a store in town when he was seventeen. He served a couple years' sentence, with his mother and father screaming about their poor baby boy the whole time. When he got out, he stuck around doing nothing at home for about four months, then tried another town and another store, and got caught coming out a back window with eight hundred dollars of cash in his jeans. He's been down at Rawlins since, and we heard five days ago that he'd broken jail. I never thought that he'd come back to these parts, though, where everybody was sure to be watching for him. I'm not sure yet. What did he look like, Annette?"

Annette gave her the description she had memorized that wild afternoon in the bus. "He had a narrow scar on his neck," she finished.

Sophie nodded. "That would be Tom. His father died a year ago, and there's just his mother and his sister Mary there now. I just hope he isn't sneaking around making it rough on them. He wouldn't care, and if he thought there was any cash around—from the settling of his dad's little old run-down ranch—he'd be after it. There couldn't be much. There's only a hundred acres, and that's not much in this country where it takes seventy acres to support a cow. Both Mrs. Nally and Mary work out for ranch women around the county when they're needed, but they know their family's never been popular and they stay to themselves otherwise. I feel sorry for Mary. The kids in town avoid her because she has a brother who is an outlaw. She must be awfully lonely sometimes." She turned away. "Got things to do. Have a look around."

Annette wandered from the stable to the barn, from there down to the wide shallow stream that meandered through the pasture, and from there back to the bunkhouse between the stable and the house. An ingenious shower house was behind the bunkhouse with a small electric pump to draw water from the stream to an overhead tank from which it showered down inside the house when needed. Life in ranch country had certainly changed, she thought, as she noted the long highline running across the country, touching down here and there at one ranch after another.

She was just turning again toward the house when a shrill nicker cut the quiet, and she turned to see the little mare still standing at the fence after the other horses had returned to pasture. Annette went to her and stood stroking the sleek neck.

"You beauty!" she breathed. "A horse of my own for the summer! The Circle Y won't be too bad."

5   *Trouble at the Line Shack*

As Annette alternately rested her tired body and sore feet and wandered about the buildings of the Circle Y, she was aware that in a quiet way the ranch was a busy place. She had heard no one give any orders to John Running, but he had backed an old tractor out of the machinery shed and spent the afternoon working on it, a mower, and a rake. Annette kept a careful distance from him and made herself a promise to keep it just as carefully for the summer, considering his indifference. He had not even appeared surprised when he had discovered they were both headed for the Circle Y.

The ranch grounds had homemade irrigation ditches leading off the shallow stream that ran down through the pasture, and she could see Sophie working along them with a hoe.

Inside the house Martha worked noisily. Finally she came to the back door and let out a hail that was answered by Sophie from the lower garden. Sophie came immediately to the machinery shed and backed the jeep up in front of the yard gate.

"Got to take Sam some supplies up at the line shack," she told Annette. "Want to ride along?"

Although Annette felt some trepidation, after the trip in the jeep yesterday, she could hardly refuse. For the next ten minutes she helped Sophie carry out various articles. There was food from the kitchen, including a lard pail of savory stew, two shirts and a pair of cotton trousers, and various medical supplies for cattle.

Contrary to the speed at which she had driven yesterday, Sophie eased the jeep across the country toward the hills on the west with expert care. Annette, clinging to the side of the seat and with the lard pail of hot stew between her feet to keep it from upsetting, was amazed at the course her cousin drove. She sent the jeep along the side of ridges, down into ravines. Although Annette was lost within minutes, it was apparent that Sophie followed a faint trail of dim wheel tracks, and that she knew exactly where she was going. The course climbed steadily upward, past outcroppings of red and yellow rocks, along the bases of buttes, the edge of rimrocks.

Assured that Sophie knew what she was doing, Annette watched the country and found it beautiful. At this higher level, stands of aspen followed the slashes, their pale undersides turning in and out so that they shivered and quaked in the wind.

They began to see cows then, many of them with big-eared calves frisking at their heels. "Looks like Sam's pulled most of 'em through," Sophie said proudly.

"Were they sick?" Annette asked.

Sophie turned from her driving long enough to give her a curious look. "Huh?" Then she chuckled. "Child, you got lots to learn! No, we're having a late calving time on the ranch this year. It began to get hot and we drove the cows about halfway up the hills so that the heat and the flies wouldn't bother too much. Sam, our other hand, has been living up at the line shack for three weeks, helping with the calving. I take him what he needs once a week."

She had driven out onto a broad shelf of land flanked with a stand of low timber. Ahead Annette saw a little cabin which seemed more and more battered the closer they approached. By the time Sophie braked before it, Annette decided that with luck it might even shed a light rain.

For a few minutes she and Sophie were busy carrying in the supplies. Inside, Sophie built a fire in the small rusty stove and set the lard pail on top of it. "Wonder where Sam is," she mused.

She was not long in finding him. Outside, she let out a loud whoop and it was answered by a rather weak hail from back in the timber. Sophie frowned and listened. "Now what's wrong with Sam?"

"What makes you think anything's wrong?" Annette asked.

"When Sam hollers, he hollers," Sophie said shortly.

At that moment a short stout man limped into sight through the trees. Annette could see that the limp came from one leg being shorter than the other, but he also had a bandage around his head below his hat brim. Sophie drew in her breath sharply and headed up the rise to meet him. Annette could see her gesturing as she asked questions, scolding as she tried to get him to sit down on a rock while she examined his head. She could also see his impatient gestures as he waved her aside and limped on down toward the cabin.

He stopped a few feet in front of Annette. "Now who are you?"

Sam had gray eyes with a gleam, a hooked nose above a short moustache—all set on a lined weathered face that had seen its share of years. His expression was humorously fierce.

"That's Annette," Sophie told him. "She's going to give us a hand this summer."

"Doesn't look like any cowhand I ever seen here before," he replied.

"Sam, sit down and let me look at this head of yours. Take your hat off. I swear! With that hat on sideways

over that bandage you look like you'd been thrown out
of someplace! Now what happened?"

"Let me eat first!" Sam protested. "Whoever gave me
that lump swiped all there was to eat around here, too.
My stomach's gratin' my backbone. If you hadn't come,
I was goin' to—" Sam suddenly sank down on a rock, his
face turning white.

Promptly Sophie pushed his head forward. "Put your
head on your knees, Sam. Shut your eyes and wait it
out. Annette, bring him some water from the bucket
inside."

In a few moments Sam got to his feet and went inside
the cabin where Sophie placed a plate of stew before
him. Below the bandage around his head, Annette could
see the faint edgings of dried blood.

"I dunno what happened," he told them as he ate. "I
was up a mite late with a cow last night, and come in
about ten o'clock. I don't remember anything, as I came
through the door, except hearing something move here
inside the cabin. Then something hit me. When I came
to, I was by myself, but my food—all of it—and my
flashlight were gone."

"What about your rifle?"

"Gone, too. Blankets off my bed, my other work-
shirt. He about cleaned me out. I can't figure who'd be
around."

Sophie was quiet a moment. "Hard telling. You been
up here for a week so you probably hadn't heard Tom
Nally's broke jail."

They exchanged a look. Sam's heavy brows lifted, then fell. He went on eating silently.

When he finished eating, Sophie, over his protests, removed the bandage from his head and examined the lump with the open cut across it. "He really beaned you," she told him. "Gather your gear and ride home with me. This needs care and there's nothing here to do it with."

Sam's fuming did him no good. When he made no move to "gather his gear," she put all the food she had brought back in the jeep, his clothes, even his hat, then turned to Annette.

"Honey, think you can ride Sam's nag in? Toby's gentle and won't give you any trouble."

With dismay Annette recalled that she had been lost when they had been a mile from home. By now Sam had given up argument, and he saw her expression. "Just give Toby his head. He'll come home."

Annette walked down across the meadow with Sophie toward a saddled brown horse on a picket line. "Don't be upset by this, Annette," Sophie said reassuringly. "I'll drive slowly and keep you in sight until we get into open country. There is somebody loose in these hills, and we won't take chances. I want Sam where I can watch him, though, with that head. He's been with us a long time, and the Circle Y is home to him. When he came here he was still getting over an injury in which a horse had fallen on him. Since then, he's been crippled. It's not always easy for women ranchers to find help, or for crippled men to find jobs—so we've made a good team."

Annette mounted and, wearing Sam's hat against the sun, set out in the wake of the jeep. Now and then Sophie stopped and waited for her to catch up, and not until they had cleared the short strips of aspen and the rock outcroppings that could hide a man, did she move away and drive on home. Although the trip seemed long, Annette found herself enjoying it, and after a mile, her sore muscles yielded to necessity.

Back at the barnyard, John Running still worked on the motor but he glanced up in surprise when she came riding in on Toby alone. At the house Annette found Sophie cleaning Sam's wound.

"I think I'll report this to the sheriff," she said aloud, "and I think we'll just keep a watch out. This makes three from our outfit who've been hit in one twenty-four-hour stretch."

When she had made the call, she paused looking up at the shotgun above the kitchen door. She took it down, cleaned it carefully, and reloaded it. Annette found herself a little shaken. Never before had she been in a household where a gun was cleaned, loaded, and ready for anything that might happen. She went in to lie down on the bed and although everything outside seemed deeply peaceful with wind blowing through the cottonwoods, hens clucking lazily, the distant ring of John's hammer, she was suddenly homesick for the gang, for Uncle Archie and Aunt Lila and the big old house in Hollywood, the giggles and chatter, the constant "Let's go somewhere!" of the crowd in summer. Then she napped.

At the table that night Martha said a matter-of-fact grace, and for a time everyone ate in silence. John sat across from Annette, never lifting his eyes from his plate although he ate with respectable manners.

Martha was the one who finally broke the silence. "How'd you get along today?"

Annette glanced up, not sure who was being addressed. "Me?"

"You."

John answered before Annette could. "She scared the stock."

"She'll learn, John," Sophie reproved.

"Got to," Martha added.

Before Annette could make an indignant reply, Sophie gave an order. "John, in the morning leave the little sorrel in the corral."

During the ensuing silence while everyone ate, Annette soothed her ruffled feelings and began wondering what they would all do with the rest of the evening.

She found out as soon as the last fork had been laid down. While she and Martha finished the dishes, Sophie built a fire in the great fireplace. She brought another rocker from one of the bedrooms, and the five of them settled in front of the fire. Sam, his freshly bandaged head showing white in the reflected firelight, nodded and dozed. John, apparently by preference, ignored his chair and stretched out on the floor on his stomach.

The sisters rested heads against their chair backs and were silent.

Annette, unused to so complete a silence, was amazed at these people. Either they had nothing to say to each other or they understood the others so entirely that there was no need for talk.

Finally she broke the quiet. "When do your people from the East come?"

"Last of June," Martha answered shortly.

After a few moments Sophie added some information. "There will be three of them—a widower with two sons, sixteen and eight. He's coming out here to finish a book he's working on. He mainly wanted to know if the place would be quiet enough for study, and he also wanted a place where his boys could spend the summer in the great outdoors."

Annette watched Sophie's face, but saw no trace of irony. "That's a nice little house you've built for them."

"Cost plenty," Martha added.

"Got to finish the outside yet," Sophie explained. "Paint and finish around the windows. We did the inside first so as to be sure and be ready. Yes, it's expensive, but we're trying for a toehold in a small way first, then we'll add a little every year in the way of equipment. John and Sam have both got what we'll need in experience, and we've got beautiful country to ride in with the Big Horns so close. Lucky for us, we've got people coming this year who don't seem to want much, so we won't have to lay in packtrain equipment for this year at least."

"Isn't the equipment expensive?" Annette asked.

"Usually you only have to lay it in once over a period of time," Sophie explained. "The professor's paying us fifty dollars a week apiece for meals, housing, a horse to ride. It's a start for a small outfit like we are."

"How much land do you have?"

"Five thousand acres," Sophie said quietly. Surprise silenced Annette. It seemed like a lot of country. "It runs up onto the lower slopes of the Big Horns, and there's government land above that that we can graze cattle on by lease and wander around over with dudes later on."

Martha rose. "There's money in dudes. Time for bed."

The two men rose and went out, headed for the bunkhouse without wasting time on good-nights. Sophie closed the door behind them, stood looking at it uncertainly for a moment.

"Lock it." Martha's tone was firm.

Sophie glanced over her shoulder. "That door hasn't been locked for thirty years."

"Good time to begin." Martha waited where she was until Sophie had made the old bolt slip home. Slowly she lifted her glance to the shotgun which she had cleaned earlier and replaced. Quietly she took it down and went to her bedroom. Watching, Annette again felt that small chill of apprehension.

When Martha's rasping voice cut the predawn darkness the next morning, Annette had to shove herself forcibly out of bed. She slipped into the jeans and blouse she had laid ready, ran a comb through her hair and reached the kitchen just as Martha opened the back door and sent a ringing whoop toward the bunkhouse. She was answered by one in return. Sleepily Annette decided that anybody at Circle Y who wanted anybody else just whooped, although how the right one appeared, she could not explain.

Martha was already frying bacon, and she spoke over her shoulder. "Set the table, lay out bread, dish up cereal."

Annette shook her head to come fully awake and Sophie, pulling on her boots, grinned at her teasingly. By the time Annette, without directions, had found and placed the items, John and Sam were waiting behind their chairs. Martha gave her usual clipped grace as though confident that at this hour of the morning not even God had time to waste. Breakfast was otherwise wordless.

When the five rose from the table, two sets of orders set the routine of the day. Martha spoke to Annette. "Clean up the kitchen, then hoe in the garden. When the dew is off the vines, pick some snap beans for dinner. After that, weed the petunias."

Sophie spoke to John and Sam. "Get the machinery in shape to start the hayfield tomorrow morning."

Annette learned in the next two hours that when Martha gave an order she expected its execution in detail. She looked up to find the tall unsmiling woman watching her use a hoe along the edges of the onion row. "You can't get the weeds that way. It takes getting on your hands and knees and using your fingers."

Annette's back was aching when she had finally finished the single row by midmorning when the sun was beating down and a hot wind was blowing in from the southwest. Annette decided only one thing could be said for gardening—there was time for thinking. The events that had brought her here seemed far away and not very important. She was even beginning to understand Uncle Archie's reasoning and see that she had asked for what had happened.

"If Uncle Archie wants something proved by this summer deal, I suppose I can give it a whirl. It can't be too bad if it's no worse than this."

She worked in the yard under the cottonwoods until Martha's hail called her inside to help with dinner. Afterward, she again straightened the kitchen, then went to the door of the living room, which, like all the rooms except the kitchen, appeared little used. "Will you please check and see if I've done things the—the way you want them."

Martha inspected, nodded. "That's all right. The day's yours now till six o'clock. Then don't forget the chickens and to bring me in a bucket of coal. Put fresh towels in the shower house."

Although she was tired, Annette felt a little restless and she wandered outdoors. Sophie was standing beside

John and Sam where they worked over the mower.

"Annette, every day saddle your mare and go get the mail down at the road. The mare's bridle is the one just inside the barn door."

Delighted, Annette plucked a withered apple from the kitchen leavings and went to the corral. The mare whinnied softly through her nose and came immediately to Annette for her treat, her ears pitched far forward in anticipation. While she ate, Annette slipped a rope around her neck and led her to a post at the side of the corral. She found the saddle, flattened the blanket on the mare's back without trouble, and lifted the saddle.

The attitude of Cindy changed as suddenly as a March wind. Instead of a friendly, quiet, appealing little mare, she was a dancing, ear-flattened, head-tossing, troublesome demon. She did not try to kick or break loose, but she kept up her dancing, curving away from the saddle as Annette approached, lips curling fiendishly back from her teeth, nose wrinkling.

Annette looked toward the tractor fifty yards away. Sophie had disappeared. John was still there, his head bent over his work. "I'm not going to call him for help!" Annette told herself. "I told Sophie I rode horseback, and ride I will!"

She paused, the heavy saddle over one arm while with her free hand she caressed the mare's neck until she quieted. Then she tried again. Cindy again showed all her demon traits.

Determined, Annette let her retreat until she was

broadside to the fence, straightened the blanket, and suddenly flung the saddle across her back. The mare squatted and jumped. The saddle slipped but Annette shoved it back in place. She glanced over the animal's back with a sense that John had seen the performance and was secretly laughing at her awkwardness.

She led the mare away from the rail fence, then reached under her to catch the trailing cinch and pulled it tight. She was immediately aware that the mare swelled and held her breath. The riding master had taught her how to handle that problem. Raising her knee, she jabbed the mare sharply in the belly so that her breath went out suddenly while the cinch was pulled tight.

As Annette stepped back in triumph, Cindy began dancing and prancing again. Annette knew the sick feeling in the pit of her stomach. She was scared.

Making herself as calm as if she rode a troublesome horse every afternoon, she reentered the barn for the bridle. All she found was a bridle with a strange contraption in place of a bit. There was nothing to go into the mouth at all.

She gave up finally and went to hunt Sophie, but Sophie had disappeared. As she passed the tractor, John looked up with a humorous glint in his eye. "Something wrong?"

"I can't find the bridle," she confessed.

"Sophie told you," he said critically. "First one inside."

"There's no bit in it," she retorted.

He gave her a look that said plainly what he was thinking. This was exactly what one could expect of a girl.

Indignantly Annette turned away. She wanted to cry with rage. *I hate him!* she told herself.

She was looking through the bridles again when a shadow darkened the door. A brown hand reached past her, lifted the first bridle down and handed it to her. "It's a hackamore. Shuts off a horse's wind if he gets funny with you. Cindy needs it." He was gone.

As she carried the bridle to the corral, Annette wondered if she had imagined the faintly victorious tone in his voice.

6 *Conquering Cindy*

Annette slipped the headstall on Cindy and studied the arrangement. It seemed an uncertain contraption, and she glanced under the mare's neck toward the tractor. John was sitting sideways to her, and she felt sure this was planned so he could view her.

She tightened her lips, gathered the reins, put her foot in the stirrup and went quickly into the saddle because she remembered the words of the riding master. "When you get on a horse, do it quickly. Don't drag yourself up and over."

Cindy stood quietly, tossing her head a little. John had left the gate open and, knees gripped, she urged the mare out through the gate and down the lane. To her surprise, the mare traveled along at a little jog, her neck arched. Annette relaxed but kept a watchful eye on those perked ears.

At the mailbox beside the road the mare pulled up alongside so that Annette could open the door. There was no mail, so she shut the door and decided to ride on down the road.

At that moment Cindy decided differently. Head bowed stubbornly down, almost to her knees, she wheeled and started for home at a determined walk. Annette pulled hard on the reins, heard the mare's breath come with a smothered sound. Cindy stopped, pushing her head forward against the bridle trying for freedom, prancing in place. For a second Annette felt a surge of fright, the feeling that her mount was preparing to toss her if possible.

The thought of John's amusement if she came back defeated stiffened her determination. *I won't walk back!*

Pulling back hard, she leaned out far enough to watch what the metal contraption on the bridle really did, and suddenly she understood. The two parts of the hackamore squeezed together at the pull of the reins so that first the horse's nostrils were shut off. Cindy's mouth was open, dragging in the air she needed. Annette pulled back hard, and saw the hackamore squeeze the mare's mouth shut so that she got air neither through mouth nor nostrils. A horse went where a rider wished because it was the only way he could breathe.

She pulled hard against that tossing head and neck-reined hard to the left, kicking Cindy in the ribs. Reluctantly, buck-jumping in anger and frustration, Cindy turned and headed down the road at a trot. A hundred yards along, however, she suddenly wheeled and started back at a gallop. By now Annette knew what she was doing. She repeated the accomplishment at the mailbox, then swung the mare around and back. Cindy half reared and Annette smothered fright and lashed her shoulder with the rein ends. Cindy dashed away down the road, and Annette relaxed the rein pressure to let her breathe. Twice in the next half mile Cindy repeated her rebellion, then gave up and walked peacefully north. Savoring her victory, Annette let her walk for a time, urged her finally to a lope and rode with a feeling of freedom and exhilaration that grew more intoxicating by the minute.

The sun beat down heavily, however, and as she came to the end of fenced land—Lowery land, she supposed—she saw a line of cottonwoods along the bank of the stream that ran from the barn on across the pasture and through this unfenced area. She took Cindy down toward it along the fence line. At the bank, Cindy splashed through without hesitation and climbed the low opposite bank, moving along under the trees of her own volition.

Under the largest cottonwood Annette pulled the

mare to a halt and sat looking about. The wind had died and there was only the babbling sound of water over rocks. The shade was soothing to her sunburned face and for a few minutes Annette sat in the saddle peering through the low leafy screen of cottonwood branches at everything that made up the pleasant scene.

Suddenly Cindy threw up her head, ears pitched to the right. From over the rise behind the trees Annette heard hoofbeats coming. Then through the leaves she saw a rider coming down the stock trail. The rider was a girl with dark hair fastened by a red ribbon at the base of her neck. She rode bareback on a rather raggedy-looking horse, and her blue jeans were worn a gray-white.

As the girl topped the rise and rode down to the stream, Cindy nickered suddenly, the sound belling shrill and clear. The girl wheeled her horse toward the sound for a startled moment, sighted Annette's mount through the cottonwood screen, yanked her horse's head around and fled up the trail and was gone.

For a moment Annette sat where she was. She would have liked to make the acquaintance of the rider, for their ages must be about the same. "You!" she told Cindy. "Why didn't you keep still?"

As she considered the location, however, she began to wonder if she were trespassing. She urged Cindy to the top of the trail and half a mile away saw the small house and barn that yesterday Sophie had said belonged to the Nally family. From a distance the spread looked shabby and run-down. The rider was just entering the barnyard, and Annette saw her slip from the horse's back and stand looking in the direction from which she had come. After a moment she led the horse inside the stable.

Annette rode back across the stream and headed along the fence line at a fast gallop, feeling a little chagrined about the whole matter. She came loping in past John, closed the corral gate, unsaddled and curried the mare before turning her loose. The fact that John had stood looking in surprise pleased her.

"He saved my life on the mountain. I saved his with the police. He gave me a bridle he didn't think I could use on a horse he was sure I couldn't manage, but I did. We're even again."

The thought was comforting whether the last half was accurate or not. As she went to the house, she decided not to say anything about the girl to her cousins. She had made enough mistakes without having them tell her to stay off neighboring land.

For the next two weeks Annette devoted herself to learning the routine, and in spite of the fact that she discovered muscles she had not known existed, she had enough fun on Cindy afternoons to more than compensate for what occasionally seemed sheer drudgery. This ranch was run by strict routine, inside and out, and it became a routine of Annette's own making that each afternoon she saddled her mount and reported to Sophie for any errands to be run. Often she rode several miles to neighboring ranches with messages. During the haying season it became her task to take fresh water to the men at midafternoon. With the machinery in full repair, the haying seemed to be a steady summer job with John and Sam busy each day and often several miles from the house. Each evening she brought in the two milk cows, and once, after some hesitation, Sophie asked her if she would ride up to summer range and see how the cattle there were doing.

"I'm wondering if maybe we should take them higher for the rest of the summer," she explained. "I don't know. Maybe you'd better not go up there."

"Why not?" Annette asked.

"Well, nobody's heard anything more about Tom Nally, but that doesn't mean—" she trailed off uncertainly.

In the end, Sophie mounted a horse herself and they rode together. When they reached the line cabin, she noticed that Sophie took a long searching look about before she dismounted, and another look inside the cabin.

"Nobody's been around," she reported as she came out. "Now let's look at the cattle and the grass."

The former were doing well; the latter was getting short with the summer dry season coming on. Sophie and Annette spent the afternoon pushing fifty head of cattle several miles higher on the slopes where the grass was greener and near where a mountain stream coursed downward toward the valley.

Annette did not miss the fact that Sophie kept a careful lookout not only ahead and around, but that she also studied the ground ahead of the cattle as they traveled behind her horse, once they had been started.

"That does it," Sophie remarked when they had gone as far as she chose.

Annette was shading her eyes with her hand and looking upward. "Isn't that Medicine Mountain?" She pointed high and to the southwest.

Sophie nodded. "I've never seen the Medicine Wheel. What's it like?"

When Annette had described the strange oval of rocks with their radiating lines, Sophie nodded. "I think I'm going to see it sometime. Mighty few of the people who live here have climbed that high or ever heard of the Wheel." Sophie had a peculiar expression on her face during the moments that the two of them sat their horses watching the drifts of white cloud slipping across the top of Medicine Mountain.

"What are you thinking about?" Annette asked her.

Sophie smiled. "Of a story a woman told me only a couple years ago. She was a naturalist, belonged to the Wyoming Historical Society. That group is pretty rugged and they take long rides and tramps through this country investigating little-known things. She said that ever since the white men came to this country—and the Indians before that—there have been reports that on occasion people have glimpsed tiny figures, human figures, up near the Medicine Wheel. The historians have not been able to come up with solid facts, but still the stories keep cropping up, and from reliable sources, too. For a couple hundred years there have been reports that at one time the mountains of Wyoming were inhabited by an underground midget race."

Annette was staring at her in fascination. "Not—not really?"

Sophie nodded. "Those stories come not only from the Medicine Wheel. People at other Wyoming locations tell yarns of seeing tiny figures slip into caverns too small for ordinary men."

"But surely people don't believe that!" Annette cried.

Sophie hesitated before replying. "Well, probably not really. Yet when the stories keep cropping up, I think historians and naturalists just keep their minds and eyes open. They have found long-ago signs of such a race, but as for their being in existence today—you can't get anybody to admit that—but neither do they deny it. It's like that."

"But it seems like superstition."

Sophie turned her horse down the mountain. "It does." She grinned at Annette over her shoulder. "You want to deny the stories?"

Annette followed her down the trail while she thought about an answer. "No," she said slowly. "I don't think I do."

As she rode, she had a remembrance of John as he had stood facing the circle of stones, his lips moving, his arms lifting. There had been his certainty, also, that because he had prayed there nothing could hurt them.

If by now Annette felt easily comfortable around Sophie, she could not say the same about Martha. How two such different women could be sisters, could occupy the same house for so many years, yet be so different, she could not understand. She did not dislike Martha; it was just that she could neither know nor understand her. Contrasting with Sophie's noisy, outgoing, warm-hearted personality, Martha was silent to grimness, her feelings hidden, her attention strictly on the routine of house, yard, and garden. At first without actually saying so, she gave Annette the feeling that most of the things she did were wrong or poorly done, but after listening to her give a dozen-word scolding to John for wearing one shirt too long, Annette decided that Martha would have no hesitation about telling her, too, if she were wrong. Thereafter, she did not worry about it.

One person she was enjoying greatly was Sam. His evening tales of early ranch days in the West held her fascinated, and it had not taken her long to realize that he could tell a preposterous joke with the sobriety with which a minister preached a sermon.

"When I was in Montana one winter, on the Turkey M, it got so cold that we didn't waste time shaving. We just wet our faces and stuck 'em out the door into the wind. When the whiskers froze we snapped 'em off with our fingers, although we howled when we did it," he told her one evening, his faraway expression deep in the crackling fire.

Annette had already been through a few of these yarns. This time she thought quickly. Maintaining the same faraway expression, she asked a quiet question.

"And I suppose nobody knew which one had howled the loudest until the howls thawed out in the spring and you could recognize voices?"

For a moment there was silence. Then Sophie snickered. John rose as wooden-faced as ever but he smote Sam a blow on the shoulder as he went out. Sam grinned sheepishly and then with admiration. "You're right!" he exclaimed. "And I had the loudest howl of anybody that spring."

One day Annette decided that instead of riding, she would put on her bathing suit and follow the creek across the pasture. Perhaps she could find a spot deep enough for some swimming. With jeans and shirt slipped on over her suit, she walked along the bank for almost a mile, then found herself at the fence line she had followed on her first ride.

She hesitated momentarily, then was determined enough to swim that she slipped under the fence and walked along under the trees. Beyond the big cotton-wood, she found a place where the water, in turning a bend, backed itself into a waist-deep pool in the shade. She hung her jeans and shirt across a protruding root, and waded into water still cold from mountain snow. When she was used to it, she floated on her back and watched the clouds.

It's funny, she thought. *I don't even seem to miss the gang.*

As she sat up, she heard splashing around the corner of the bank. Quietly she rose and moved to where she could see over the bank. The girl she had seen before was there, standing thigh deep in water as she flung a stick to a brown dog bounding joyously up and down in the stream. He almost flung himself across the stream, half swimming, half leaping, up the opposite bank to retrieve the stick. Spray plumed out in every direction as he leaped back in and swam toward the girl, who laughed in delight. She flung the stick again, and as the dog left she dropped down into the water to her chin to wait.

Deliberately Annette got to her feet. "Hi there!"

The girl gasped in surprise, floundered to her feet, and stood staring with her mouth open. "H-Hello," she said faintly.

Then it was Annette's turn to be surprised, for the girl wheeled, traveling in great leaps to clear the water, and dashed a few yards downstream, climbed the bank, and with water spraying back from her clothes fled up the trail with the dog in pursuit.

Annette sank back into the water in dismay. "Now what did I do to her?"

Somehow the pleasure had gone out of the afternoon. Climbing out of the water, she slipped her jeans and shirt on over her wet bathing suit and headed for home, feeling a little rejected.

She found Sophie in the corral trying to persuade a cow with her first calf to accept it. Annette watched from the top of the fence as Sophie placed the calf alongside her. The cow kicked and she pulled the calf hastily back, tried again. The business took half an hour, but at the end the animal accepted her progeny as though it were a fine surprise she had been planning the whole time. Sophie's weathered face creased in a pleased grin as she stepped back and came over to the fence.

"Sophie, should I not go beyond the north-pasture fence?"

Sophie's blue glance came up with instant reaction. "What's happened?"

Annette told her of meeting the girl when she was riding, of what had happened today when she had gone swimming.

Sophie was silent a moment. "Mary Nally, poor kid. Poor lonely misfit youngster!"

"But what's wrong with her? I just wanted to get acquainted. She acted scared."

"I suppose she is. It started when her brother Tom got in trouble the first time. Despite all we say about children being little angels, they aren't. The day Tom was caught, a group of boys on their horses went out at night and rode circles around their house, yelling, among other things, 'Jailbird! Jailbird!' At that time Mary was about fourteen years old, and her mother told me the incident almost scared her to death. She's never forgotten it. She's no coward though—except where people are concerned."

"But she goes to school, doesn't she? She'd meet people there and some of them would treat her all right, wouldn't they?"

Sophie sighed. "That didn't work either. Mary probably either didn't meet or didn't let herself meet the right ones. The others made slighting remarks they made sure she overheard, and the right ones didn't try too hard to do anything about it.

"Anyway, Mary dropped out of high school late in her freshman year. She just couldn't take it anymore. Her mother worked for me two winters ago, when Marthy had pneumonia, and she said she couldn't persuade her to go back. Neither could the probation officer. When he came out the second time to enforce the school ruling, Mary wasn't there. She's a ranch child, and she knows plenty of places in this country to hide—like the old-time trappers. Finally, the authorities have just let it slide."

"But, what does she do with herself?"

"As I told you a while back, her father died a year ago. She and her mother run that little ranch—a few cows, a few sheep, and her mother works out when there's work. So does Mary. They manage. People talk about seeing Mary up in the hills with her old horse and her dog, never anybody with her. That's her entertainment, I suppose."

They stood together for a few quiet moments. "I think

I'll go to see her. Just plain go to the house and make her acquaintance."

Sophie gave her a surprised look. "Well, I don't know what kind of reception you'll get. Mary's full of barbs, and if she's cornered, I imagine she knows how to use them where they'll hurt the most."

She decided not to carry out her decision, however, until the swimming incident would be forgotten. Meanwhile, life at the ranch continued its busy round with a few puzzling incidents added for thought. One night a chicken squawked in the chicken house, followed by wild fluttering, flapping and more squawking. Badger, the deaf old Circle Y collie, came ranting out of the stable and went tearing out across the pasture to the north.

By then, everyone was up, and Sophie was standing outside the back door with the shotgun in her hand. John, bare from his blue jeans up, came racing to her. "Let me have it, Miss Sophie! I'll trail him down. I heard him runnin'! I'll—"

"No, you won't, John," Sophie told him. "I know what you'd do. You'd shoot him down, then be in trouble with the police again."

"But he'd have it comin'! Come on, please."

Sophie stoutly put the gun behind her back. "He has it coming but not from you, John. I know the law. I can defend my place, because I own it. You can't and you're to blame for killing anybody for that reason. You've had enough law trouble now."

With a gesture of irritation, John had run off into the darkness just as a pained series of yelps sounded half a mile across the pasture.

Fifteen minutes later John returned carrying the old dog with a badly cut head from which blood dripped. John set the dog down on the kitchen floor, and his fingers, oddly gentle, probed the three-inch cut with bruised edges. Badger whined, but he endured the gentle fingers.

"Coyotes," Sophie said quietly.

John's head raised slowly. "You know better'n that, Miss Sophie. I know a fang slash from a club blow. So do you."

7   *The Haunted Bunkhouse*

A week later Annette brought Sophie a letter from the mailbox, and at the supper table that night Sophie made an announcement. "Our dudes are arriving two weeks from Sunday."

Martha straightened. "Means I got to finish up the guesthouse."

"And I," Sophie added, "will have to finish getting the wiring installed. That'll be half a day's work."

Sam looked up at Sophie from under his heavy brows. "What do those dudes expect to do out here?

More than that, what are we goin' to do with the dudes?"

From the wise look in Sam's eye, Annette guessed that he knew more about dudes and their ways than Sophie did. It was something she had been wondering about herself.

The expression on Sophie's square features was one of annoyance. "The professor wants to work on his book and he wants his boys outdoors. We furnish the meals, the quarters, and horses."

As Sam continued to eye her, she snapped at him. "Got any better ideas, Sam?"

"Nary an idea! Will his boys fall in with the professor's plans? This is a ranch, not a dude ranch. Who's to look after them kids while John an' me are workin'?"

Sophie's reply left Annette thunderstruck. "Annette will. She's the age of the older boy. She's surprised us by managing horses so well, and none of the trails around here are dangerous until you get into the mountains. What she can't handle, the rest of us will fill in."

Annette dropped her fork with a clatter. "But, I'm not up to—what you're expecting!"

"Certainly you are. As of next week we are putting you on the ranch payroll." Sophie rose, the conversation finished.

In bed that night Annette assessed the situation. A boy of sixteen was not going to take directions from a girl his own age happily, and his kid brother, at eight, probably disliked girls of any age. Sophie did not realize that dudes were entertained with rides, song-

fests, wiener roasts, hikes, and anything else within
reason that they might want.

"That girl, Mary Nally," she mused as she stared at
the ceiling and a coyote yodeled in the distance. "If I
could just make her acquaintance, maybe she'd help."

The next day she jogged Cindy toward the Nally
lane with growing misgivings. Mary Nally had already
fled her presence twice. Once Annette almost turned
the horse back, then with new-found courage she went
on.

The Nally lane showed few wheel tracks, and the
weathered swaybacked buildings had slumped haphaz-
ardly under the cottonwoods. The yard, however, was
neat and a well-tended garden stretched behind it. A
raggedy brown horse nickered welcome from the corral.

The sound brought the opening of the house door as
Annette tied Cindy. Mary Nally waited without welcome, her hand holding the doorknob as if to close it
hastily if necessary.

Annette introduced herself. "I'm Annette—from
down at the Circle Y."

"Howdy." Mary neither moved from her spot nor
invited Annette in.

It helped to have been warned that this girl had
barbs. Annette did not retreat. "I thought it would
be nice if we got acquainted. May I come in?"

Mary's lips parted uncertainly, then she held open the
screen door. The tiny house probably contained no
more than three rooms and everything Annette could

see was old and worn. The kitchen range was going and a man's blue work-shirt lay across the ironing board.

Annette smiled. "May I sit down?"

"Oh, sure. Sit here." Mary pulled a chair from the table hastily. As she noted Annette's gaze on the ironing board, she caught the shirt off it and dropped it hurriedly into a basket.

"Cousin Martha says you've lived here a long time," Annette said, hunting for a way to set this girl at ease.

"I've lived here all my life." Mary seated herself across the table, and Annette saw that her clasped hands were white around the knuckles. Quickly Mary put them under the table.

In the silence that followed Annette felt a desperate need to get conversation started. Maybe the best way was saying what she wanted. "I see you have a horse. Maybe we could take some afternoon rides together— if you're not busy. I work until two every afternoon."

The corners of Mary's mouth twitched nervously. "Why? Where would we go?"

"I'm going to have to take care of some summer guests for my cousins. I thought maybe you could show me some of the trails up into the hills—rides I could use."

There was an almost imperceptible change in the girl, a startled widening of the eyes, a stiffening of her frame. "I'd have to ask Mother. She's not here now."

Annette had been taking in details of this girl, her creamy skin, the dark brown hair tied in a ponytail,

the large brown eyes with their odd trick of widening and narrowing slightly. She was of medium height and build.

Annette rose. "Why don't you ask your mother if you could ride tomorrow, and I'll ride down and find out?"

Mary seemed relieved that her guest was leaving, and as Annette reined Cindy away, she turned to wave. Mary Nally lifted her hand indifferently and Annette left with the feeling that she had broken the ice but accomplished little—unless Mrs. Nally proved more agreeable than her daughter.

Sophie had just finished putting a ceiling light fixture in the bunkhouse and a switch button beside the door, a task she had mentioned that morning that she might as well do while wiring the guesthouse. "Give me a hand, Annette. Get the vacuum cleaner and give this place a drubbing."

The only place to attach the cord of the cleaner was to the ceiling fixture. Annette was not through when Sophie came back. "Marthy needs groceries. Come help carry. We'll finish when we get back."

Annette snapped off the light switch at the door, and soon she was off on another hair-raising ride with Sophie at the wheel. They were on their way home again by five o'clock, but halfway there a tire blew out. Dark had fallen before they walked into the kitchen where Sam and John were awaiting the supper Martha would not serve until the rest of her family returned.

Within an hour the men headed for the bunkhouse. Then the women heard a startled yell. Hurriedly Sophie snapped on the yard light in time to see the two men disentangling themselves on the ground before the bunkhouse door from which a noisy whirring sounded. John struggled to his feet and sprinted a dozen yards away into the gloom as the women hurried down the walk.

Sam sat up, rubbing his head. "He jumped back an' knocked me flat. What's that racket?"

Annette's hands went to her cheeks. "The vacuum cleaner! I forgot to disconnect it from the ceiling fixture!"

Sam climbed awkwardly to his feet, staring sourly out at John. Suddenly he chuckled. Then he clutched his ribs and roared. Sophie had pulled the cord loose, screwed in the bulb and turned the light on by now. She came out carrying the cleaner. Sam pointed from it to John and went into another uncontrollable fit of laughter.

Sophie's lips were twitching. "Shut up, Sam! You'll make things worse!"

Sam was beyond thinking. "Johnny—boy, you'll be a—a long time livin' this down! Scared of a vacuum cleaner!"

John wheeled into the darkness, his heels hitting hard. "Oh, Sophie! He's mad. I'm sorry!" Annette exclaimed.

"No more your fault than mine," Sophie told her. "I thought we'd be back earlier."

Annette started after John. "Maybe I can talk to him—"

"Don't waste your time. John's superstitious. Now he's embarrassed because of a vacuum cleaner. He'll have to get over it in his own time and his own way."

Annette, however, could not forget the baleful look he had shot at her. He was gone two days, during which she took his place in the hayfield driving the tractor and pitching hay to the best of her ability because she knew the sisters were worried that they might have lost a valued hand.

"Where do you think he's gone?" she asked Sophie.

"Probably up to the Medicine Wheel. He makes a trip every summer and he probably views it that there's no better time than now, as much of a believer in spirits as he is. I think he'll be back."

He was, but for days he refused to act as though Annette were even present.

On the first day of his return she rode to the Nallys, and a comely tired-looking woman opened the door. "I came to see if Mary could ride with me today," Annette told her.

The woman looked puzzled. "Mary? She isn't here, and she didn't tell me— Who are you?"

Realizing that Mary must not have even mentioned her, Annette introduced herself. "She was going to ask your permission."

Mrs. Nally's eyes narrowed thoughtfully. "That's nice of you to ask her. She needs company. Come with me."

At the corner of the house she pointed out to Annette the cottonwood grove where she had found Mary before. "I think"—Mrs. Nally was stopped momentarily by an attack of coughing—"that you'll find her there."

At the rise that overlooked the bank and the stream, she slowed Cindy and looked over. Below, where the stream was shallow, Mary lay stomach down in the water in her shirt and jeans. Her brown dog lay stretched on his side in the sun a few feet away. Mary's arms were folded across the end of a half-submerged log and she pillowed her head on them.

Slipping to the ground Annette tied Cindy, then walked quietly down the bank without the girl or the dog hearing her. "Hello," she said quietly.

Water surged as Mary abruptly sat up, her dark eyes wide, startled, without welcome.

"You forgot to ask your mother, so I just came anyhow." Slipping off her boots, she slid down into the water at the other end of the log, crossed her arms and leaned her head on them as Mary had been doing. "Um-m-m. That sun feels good."

Although she closed her eyes, she was well aware that for a moment Mary sat where she was, then half rose. *She's going to leave!*

Then after a pause, Mary slowly slid back into the water and Annette peeked enough to see that she laid her head as she had before. "The sun's hot but it feels good," she said.

An hour later they rode back to the Nally house

with Mary riding double behind Annette. "Could you ride tomorrow?" Annette asked as the girl dropped to the ground at the gate.

Mary turned toward the house with only the briefest of upward glances. "I guess so."

It was the extent of an hour's conversation. As Annette rode away she was conscious of more coughing inside the house.

Annette galloped home with her clothes drying in the wind of Cindy's motion. Now she realized that she felt not only the need of companionship, but that she was a little stubborn about Mary's refusal to face her school situation.

"Would I face it if I were in her shoes?"

She knew, however, that in her case, things would be different. Aunt Lila and Uncle Archie would see that she did face it, the way they had a year ago when she'd had algebra trouble and tried to drop the course. "Buckle down and learn it, Annette!" Uncle Archie had ordered. She had done just that—faced down the equations and polynomials and passed the course.

"That's what Mary isn't getting, and her mother is letting her hide from it because that's easiest for both of them."

Conversation on their ride the next day was almost as sparse as before. Mary, sitting an ancient saddle on her brown horse, headed across the sagebrush flat toward the benchland above, and within an hour they were climbing. She sat her horse with a lithe ease that Annette envied. Her head was high, her shoulders straight and a little square. The brown horse was better on closer inspection, homely and rangy rather than old, and he moved with a long easy step that made little Cindy patter to keep the pace.

Once in the foothills Annette looked down to see the country spread like a panorama with stock and game trails cutting the sage and following the contours of the land. Finally Mary pulled up beside a spring that flowed from beneath a rock. Wordlessly they drank, and Annette, determined not to be bothered by silence, dropped down on her back and watched the clouds scudding above.

Fifteen minutes later Mary broke the silence. "Why did you want to ride with me?"

8 *Coyote Chase*

Prepared for anything, Annette answered promptly. "Because it seemed silly for you and me, both of us sixteen, to live less than a mile apart for a summer and not get acquainted. Sophie told me how old you were after I saw you at the creek that first time."

Mary's lips twitched without humor. Her expression was suspicious. "What else did she say about me?"

Annette did some quick thinking. Under Mary's level gaze there was little chance to dodge issues. "She said you'd dropped school because of your brother and because of what the kids did and said. She said your dad died last winter, that you and your mother were running your ranch alone now."

"Why should you want to know me then?" Mary asked bluntly.

Again it was the time to say just the right thing, that and no more. She made her reply indifferently casual. "Because as far as your brother is concerned, I couldn't care less. You and I are the only two of an age in the neighborhood. Why let outside things spoil what could be a nice summer?"

Mary made no reply, but her gaze was far away on the country below. Finally she rose and swung up on Bullet. "Let's ride on. I just wanted you to know about me. I don't want it the way it's been before, starting out fine—oh, just great!—then having someone find out the whole story and—well, here I am again!"

During the two weeks before the summer guests came, Annette spent all the time available to her trying to further her acquaintance with this strange girl. Without intending to do so, Sophie aided the project.

"Run in the extra horses," she told John.

Later in the day she took Annette to the corral where three other horses were now penned with Cindy. "Annette, if you're going to be in charge of showing these people around, you'd better be acquainted with what they are going to ride. Meet White-Eye. He's gentle, smart, a solid citizen unless he thinks he's being misused.

Then he lets a rider know it. Probably the older boy can handle him."

She left the brown horse standing with the rope dropped and walked across the corral to a small horse with a blaze-face. "This is Piebald. The younger boy can use him. He's gentle but he's quick." She pointed to the other horse. "I don't know whether the professor plans to ride or not, but if he does that mare would be a good one. That's Mabel."

Mabel turned her head, flattened her ears, and nipped at Sophie, who slapped her good-humoredly. "Thinks she's mean, but she isn't." She turned seriously to Annette. "We don't have a lot of horses, and none of them, except maybe your Cindy, are anything very special. Don't let anyone ride Cindy. She could be ruined pretty easily. Don't let any of these people abuse any of my horses. Report it to me if they do—that is, if you can't manage the situation. Ride them all, and know what they can do, how they act, so you can tell people."

"Why would anybody abuse them?" Annette asked.

Sophie considered. "Dudes probably don't intend to, but from what I've heard, sometimes there's a lot about horses they don't know. They've ridden a little, think they know a lot, and to them a horse is like a car. They think it can travel on endlessly at a steady rate of speed. Don't let anyone get away with that, Annette. I'm putting my horses in your hands."

Impressed with her responsibility, Annette made the most of the opportunity, riding the horses in turn, sometimes taking an extra one for Mary to ride. She watched Mary's riding and tried to imitate it, realizing that in ease and dexterity she still had a long way to go.

She had been at the Circle Y almost a month when something again broke into the chicken pen one night and made off with another hen. Annette knew nothing about it until she heard the shotgun blast in the middle of the night, went into the hall to see Sophie standing in the door firing down toward the pen.

"Don't know whether it's man or coyote," she commented as Annette moved up at her shoulder.

When Sam and John reported a few minutes later, Sam told her that there were coyote tracks around the pen. Sophie shrugged. "Rather that than what I was afraid it might be," she remarked as she put the shotgun up over the door again.

The incident reminded Annette that for almost three weeks nothing had been heard about Tom Nally. For ten days after the story of his escape had become known, officers had appeared every day or so to see if the Lowery ranch had been disturbed. Reports had gone out over radio and television, and there had been several articles in the local newspaper, stating that patrols were out in the hill country. Then all had gradually died down. Sophie no longer took the shotgun to her bedroom at night, but she continued to lock the door. After a week she forgot about warning Annette not to ride alone into the hills.

Meanwhile Annette made the most of her acquaintance with Mary. Conversation remained reserved and intermittent, but Mary seemed glad that she came. Annette found herself increasingly interested in the girl, and she noticed the way she had of lifting her eyes toward the mountains as though something ominous there drew her attention, as though she could not help herself.

One day she and Mary were sitting on the Nally doorstep when a car drove into the yard. A man with a sheriff's badge leaned out the window. "May I talk to you for a minute, Mary?"

Mary's eyes widened stormily, and Annette slipped to the backyard to avoid embarrassing her by overhearing. When the car drove away, Mary came around the corner of the house. "Why do they think Tom's hanging around *here*—waiting to be caught?" A frustrated sob shook her.

"I'm sorry, Mary. I wish I could do something."

"I wish I could, too! He's my brother, but I wish he was back in jail. Then Mom wouldn't get so upset when they come. I'm glad she isn't here today." Mary struck the side of the house a hard blow with her fist.

Together they walked over to the dilapidated old yard swing and for the first time Mary talked. "Actually Mom and Dad made Tom what he is. Mom babied him and both excused him, even when he robbed that store in town the first time. Mom insisted it was unfair to send a boy to the penitentiary even though Tom was twenty-one." Unconscious of her act, she raised her eyes to the mountains again, and Annette wondered if Tom Nally still hid up there.

Two days later she rode to Nallys to find the house closed. The old car was in the shed and Mary's horse in the corral but no one answered her knock at the door. As she finished knocking the second time she heard a board creak inside the house, and a curtain at the nearest window swayed slightly.

Suddenly Annette had to control an impulse to wheel and run for her horse. Instead she walked leisurely to Cindy and rode away casually. She didn't look back at the house, but she had a feeling of being watched. For some reason the Nally women had not wanted visitors today.

By now only a week remained before the arrival of the summer guests. Sophie and Martha were busy, the first with putting the rolled-log siding on the outside of the guesthouse and the second with furnishing the inside with the accessories to make it homelike. Too busy to pause, Sophie sent Annette up to summer range to check the welfare of the cattle there.

"It's dry down here. See what the grass is doing up there. Also look for sick and injured cattle."

Feeling proud to have her judgment trusted, Annette had almost reached the high rampart that shut summer range away from the higher peaks when she heard a monotonous persistent bawling ahead. Five minutes later she came upon a cow at the base of a great round boulder. The cow wheeled, stamping lightly to warn horse and rider away. Keeping a careful distance, Annette circled the boulder until she saw a disassembled set of four small legs and a head that had been thrust back beneath the edge of the rock.

At first she thought coyote or cougar had done the work until she saw that the head and limbs had been cleanly severed. Suddenly she had that same sense of fear she had known yesterday in the Nally yard. Wheeling Cindy, she sent her flying toward home.

"Sophie, could Tom Nally still be hiding up there?" she asked when she reported her find.

The woman shook her head. "Not if he has good sense. As heavily as he's been hunted by posses, and with a reward on his head—not he! Every rancher loses a few calves a year to men who just don't want to work for a living."

From her first acquaintance with Mary, Annette had known the girl's riding skill was excellent and that Bullet had speed and endurance beyond the ordinary, but she did not know how complete both were until she rode with Mary to look at the dozen Nally cattle up on the benchland.

They had turned a corner and come upon a pair of coyotes trying to close in on a newly born calf whose mother stood near it looking first at the calf, then at the coyotes. Without a second's hesitation Mary spurred Bullet past Annette and settled on the trail of the bigger coyote as he darted and dodged in an attempt to escape.

Cindy reared as Bullet swept past, then bounded after him plunging and tugging at the bridle until Annette let her go. As the little mare caught up with Bullet, Annette saw Mary leaning from the saddle to lash the coyote with her quirt while Bullet paced the beast's every rush to escape.

Suddenly the coyote dashed to the right directly in front of Cindy. Unable to stop as her legs tangled him, the little mare stumbled, recovered, then fell over him in a drawn out, plunging spill that flung Annette finally over her head in a rolling sprawl that ended against a sage clump.

Mary was off her horse and down beside her before Annette, the breath knocked out of her, could sit up. "Annette! Oh, Annette, are you hurt?"

Annette, struggling to drag air into her lungs, sat up dazedly. She shook her head to clear it. Mary pushed her back, held her down firmly. "Lie still. Let's see if anything's broken."

When Mary had gone over her arms and legs, Annette sat up. "I'm all right." She gave a shaky giggle, then sobered as Mary sank slowly back to a sitting position, her reserved face seeming almost to crumble. Suddenly she dropped her face in her hands. Her shoulders shook silently.

"I—I saw—your horse—go down! I—I thought you were dead. You hit—that sage root—so *hard*. I thought you were dead."

The tears came in a flood. Annette, distressed, but

even more astonished, could only sit beside the girl and hold the tight shaking shoulders. "Don't! Don't cry. Everything's all right."

The deluge, now that it had finally broken loose, was hard to stop. For several minutes Mary sobbed like a brokenhearted child, until finally Annette, herself unaccustomed to quite so strong a display of emotion, could not help feeling that there was more involved than just tears over an accident.

Finally Mary sat back, wiping her eyes. "We won't chase coyotes again!"

Annette giggled. "Why not? That was fun. I'll remember this all next winter when I'm hammering away at geometry."

Mary was staring out across the valley below, and she spoke with such sudden aggressiveness that Annette's mouth fell open. "No, you won't! You'll forget everything that's happened this summer as soon as you're gone!"

"Why, I won't either!" Annette sputtered. "I'm going to remember every single thing that happened this whole summer. I didn't want to come, but now I'm glad I did."

Mary was making a determined effort to mend the ravages of tears. "I—I hope you won't. I hope you won't forget me, anyhow. I don't know how to say things very well, but the last three weeks have been the only time in my life that I had to run around with anybody." She was still gazing out at the valley, avoiding looking directly at Annette. "It's—it's certainly been different. Why did you come?"

Annette was puzzled. "What do you mean—why did I come?"

"You said you were glad you came, but that you hadn't wanted to. What made you come then?"

Annette thought about the reason and suddenly chuckled. So far, she had never talked to anyone about Uncle Archie's wrath which had brought her to the Circle Y. Now the reason seemed funny—and not very important. She told Mary then about the expensive dress and about Uncle Archie standing in the middle of the living room waving the bill in a fit of temper.

As Mary listened a totally unfamiliar slow grin spread across her face. Suddenly she dropped her head on her pulled-up knees and laughed and laughed. "I—I can just—see him!"

Annette realized that part of Mary's uncontrollable laughter was reaction from her earlier stormy and unaccustomed tears, but when the girl lifted her head her face was oddly serene and relaxed.

"Maybe someday you will," Annette said thoughtfully. "Uncle Archie's a dear. I love him and he loves me, and as I look back at the whole thing, I really don't blame him. All that money for one dress. Wow! Sometimes you have to get away from things to know just how silly they look."

Mary was silent a moment. "It must be nice to be able to get far enough from something to see how it looks. That hasn't happened to me yet. Tell me more about how you live in Hollywood."

Although a little surprised, Annette caught the cue and began chattering about the slumber parties, the classes in high school, gathering later at the Choc Shop for Cokes and conversation. Mary dropped her chin on her hands and listened, her expression absorbed. Belatedly it came to Annette that she was chattering too much about herself, about a way of life Mary had never known and probably never would.

Abruptly she changed the subject. "Mary, why don't you finish high school? You owe yourself that much. A person can hardly get any kind of job without a diploma."

Mary's reply was immediate and bitter. "What makes you think I could get one around here with or without a diploma? Anything besides work in somebody's kitchen."

"But you're thinking of that crowd of kids your own age. The older people—the ones who run businesses and shops—they wouldn't be like that so long as you had enough education to be qualified."

"You think so? They're not much better than the kids. I wouldn't risk it! I'd love to finish high school if it was just for the studies. I liked to study—although I don't believe the teachers thought I did. They tried to help, but the year that I was in high school, I was so worried about Tom, I couldn't settle down to it much. It just wasn't any use. That was after Dad was taken sick. Mom was working—anything she could get —to buy me the clothes and things I needed just to stay in school. It wasn't worth what it was costing her in effort for me to have to go and listen to the catty remarks in the school hallways, the whispers in the classrooms."

Mary dropped her head on her knees and a shiver ran through her.

"What happened to your father?" Annette asked.

"He developed heart trouble from a number of things. Trying to make our little old ranch pay, trying to work at other jobs to get enough cash just to support us, trying to keep Tom straightened out. Dad was just beginning to get on his feet when Tom went haywire and was sent to the penitentiary for a few years. He had hit a man over the head when he broke into that store, and people had a lot of things to say about the whole thing."

"Like what?" Annette asked.

"Oh, that Tom had been spoiled, and the folks had indulged him—that sort of thing. Some of it was probably true, too, but Tom would have been hard to handle no matter what. Anyhow, right after he was caught Dad had his first heart attack.

"Then Tom was sentenced and sent to Rawlins. On the evening of that day, with Dad in bed and only Mother and I here, the boys who belong to the riding club in town came out here after dark on their horses. They rode circles around the house, right through the yard yelling and hooting. The things they shouted!

They'd broken down the fence. One smashed the window of Dad's bedroom when he rode past. That was when Dad got out of bed, even when Mother and I tried to hold him down. He got his rifle and went outside. He fired into the air. I know he fired *up* because I was standing right behind him. He did it just to scare them away.

"They ran then, but they reported to the sheriff that Dad had tried to shoot one of them. The next day the sheriff was out with a warrant—made out by the father of one of the boys—for Dad's arrest. By then Dad was in bed again, sicker than before, and they couldn't take him. He died two weeks later."

Annette, listening, shocked and sickened at the story, watched Mary's face. Her voice had fallen to a level, almost monotonous, tone as she talked.

"Mary, that's awful! I'm so terribly sorry."

Mary's voice was a little weary. "It was more than I could stand—all that and the things the kids at school said. Much as I'd like to graduate, I won't go back." She was silent for a moment. She frowned. "There's only one thing—I'm worried about Mom."

"Why?"

Mary drew a deep breath before going on. "I don't think she's well. She coughs a lot ever since she had that heavy cold last winter. She's getting thinner and I know she isn't very strong. She's been working out for other ranch wives for several years, but lately she's felt so poorly that I've been going in her place. I'd hoped

I could make enough so she wouldn't have to go at all but there just isn't that much work."

"But—will you be able to keep the ranch going?"

"Not unless both of us work steadily. There was enough from Dad's insurance to pay the taxes and his doctor bills and expenses, and leave us a little. But next year—I just don't know."

For the first time since she had wept, she looked directly at Annette. "I'm scared, Annette!"

"But in spite of everything, whether you like it or not, don't you think you ought to try and finish high school somehow?"

Mary's look was challenging and direct. "Would you?"

Annette did not bother to answer, and Mary gave her faint ironic smile that was too old for her years. "You've got a lot of confidence I don't have. I've never been to a slumber party, or a prom, or out of this valley." She got to her feet. "But I've got a date to milk our cow within an hour and we've got to walk a quarter of a mile to catch our horses. Let's go."

Cindy seemed none the worse for her tumble and the girls were home within the hour driving the cow ahead of them. As Annette reined Cindy around to leave, Mary gave her a wan smile.

"Keep your spirits up," Annette told her. "Something good will happen. You'll see. It's got to."

As she rode home Annette could not help wondering, though, what could possibly be done to help Mary Nally if she refused to help herself.

9   *The Dudes*

There were three more busy days of preparation before the arrival of Professor George Way and his two sons. Martha finished the inside of the guesthouse, and Sophie had already finished the outside and set a yard chair in front of it. The last of the curtains had been hung, the big rug Martha had been braiding for weeks lay on the floor, a table was set up for the professor's typewriter, and the beds were made up and waiting.

On the morning when Sophie was to meet the bus at Stone Gulch, she lectured Sam and John. "Now, listen, you fellows, see that you come to the table in clean shirts and looking your best."

Sam's tone was dry. "There's an old gun belt in my trunk. You want I should wear it?"

John glanced up and his eye caught Annette's. There was a definite twinkle there. Apparently the incident of the vacuum cleaner was fading. "I got two pair of spurs —great big rowels. I could wear one to breakfast and the other to supper."

Sophie gave them an indignant look. "I mean it, boys."

After breakfast she backed out an old station wagon which Annette had never seen her drive before. Together they dusted it out thoroughly.

"Well, two hours now," Sophie commented. "Get your riding boots polished, Annette, and get all slicked up."

"But, I thought I'd wear a dress," Annette protested.

"Oh, no," Sophie protested. "Put on your riding clothes. You've got those good-looking boots. You look cute in your jeans and with Sam's hat."

Although it was not exactly Annette's idea of the way to start, she did as she was asked and rode into Stone Gulch with Sophie wearing a dress for the first time since Annette had known her. With her short almost man-cut hair, she was astonishingly unfamiliar.

As the big bus pulled into the station Annette saw a boy rush to the exit door. He hopped to the ground and looked about eagerly. He was about eight years old, freckled above a grin that was apparently habitual.

"Hey, did you come to meet us?" he demanded as Sophie and Annette moved forward. "I'm Ronnie Way."

Before they could do more than nod, a tall man in glasses descended and turned. He had a serious, thoughtful expression. His shoulders were slightly stooped and he was so lean that his clothing seemed to hang. He made Sophie a little bow. "You are Miss Lowery?"

"I am, and you are Professor Way," she replied as though it were a foregone conclusion.

He turned as a youth stepped down from the bus, a suitcase in his hand. He was slender and dark, more neatly dressed than his father and brother and with a faint spattering of freckles across his face.

"This is Kevin," Professor Way informed them.

Sophie held out her hand, and Kevin touched it unsmilingly. "This is Annette," Sophie said as she touched her hand to Annette's arm. "Annette's our right-hand girl around the place. Come! The car's this way."

With Ronnie trotting ahead of them, the five moved toward the station wagon. The professor was chatting about the country. "This is going to be wonderful. Simply wonderful!" he exclaimed. "I don't know how I had the good sense to make such a fine plan for the summer."

There was such a sharp contrast between Ronnie's eagerness, the professor's enthusiasm, and Kevin's critical silence that Annette stole a sidewise look at Kevin as the three men climbed into the back of the station wagon. He settled in a seat, glanced at his watch, then looked indifferently out the window.

I wonder if he'd recognize us if he saw us again, Annette thought. *Maybe he's just tired.*

All the way home the professor was asking questions of Sophie, admiring the country, exclaiming at the herds of cattle and a horse running across a pasture with his tail plumed high. Ronnie meanwhile was deluging Annette with questions.

"What's my horse like? How soon can we ride? Where do we go? Do you have cattle on your ranch? How many horses are there? Will we go up to those mountains over there?" One at a time, double, or triple, they boiled out of the boy, and while Annette and Sophie cut across each other's conversations with father and son, the other son sat silent and evidently was not even listening. Because he made no effort to even look at any of them, Annette carefully kept her glance from him and talked to Ronnie.

Once at home Sophie introduced the guests to Martha, who managed to shed her dour expression long enough to give them a welcome, then took them to the guesthouse to unpack. "Lunch in half an hour," she informed them.

As Annette helped Martha in the kitchen, the woman asked her a single question. "What do you think of them?"

Surprised at having this particular cousin ask for an opinion from one as inexperienced as herself, Annette was slow to reply. "I think we've got one problem."

Martha turned back to the stove. "Me, too."

Lunchtime was a continuation of the conversation on the way home. Both the cousins cast occasional sidelong glances at Kevin, who ate lightly and paid no attention to any of them.

"I'll take care of the dishes," Martha told Annette. "See what you can do for what ails that one."

The hammer of a typewriter was already coming from the guesthouse as Annette went across the yard, and the two boys were just coming out. "Would you like to look around?" she asked.

"You bet!" Ronnie exclaimed, already headed for the yard gate.

"I suppose so," Kevin replied. The corner of his mouth quirked faintly in something that was not really a smile at all, as though he was trying to be agreeable about something in which he had scant interest.

By the time they reached the corral where the horses were held, Ronnie was up on the rail looking down at them. "Which is mine?"

"Yours is the piebald," Annette told him. "That's his name—Piebald."

Kevin made his first voluntary contribution. "And what's a piebald?"

"A horse with a lot of spots. It looks as though he's gotten spattered with paint," Annette explained.

Kevin made a disinterested sound and stood looking through the rails, hands in his pockets, swaying a little on the balls of his feet. Annette would have considered him a handsome boy if his face were not twisted by his dour expression.

Kevin improved on his brief conversational record. "The other little one—that's mine, I suppose?"

Annette set him straight quickly. "No, that's Cindy, and she's mine. Yours is White-Eye, the tall horse."

"He's got a blind eye," Kevin observed.

"No, it isn't," Annette told him. "It's just white. Horsemen say a horse with a white eye never goes blind."

Kevin shrugged. "I say he's blind. He's a homely brute, but if that's the way it is—" He turned away and strolled toward the stable and machine shed.

Annette followed. "Have you ridden much?"

He answered over his shoulder. "Go to a riding academy off Central Park sometimes."

By now he had reached the bunkhouse. Sam had left the door open that morning as usual. Kevin glanced inside. "Who lives here?"

"The two hands, Sam and John."

For the first time he turned and gave her a straight glance. "You mean they make their help sleep in a shed outside the house? I thought that was just in the movies —in the old days."

It was strange how a certain tone of voice could suddenly make something one had taken for granted seem all wrong. Annette looked at the neat small building. True, it could stand a coat of paint. Inside, it was furnished with old things from the house but they were comfortable things, two rockers, a table with hunting and sports magazines, shelves for the men's belongings, a good closet.

She found herself defending the situation. "Bunkhouses are the same on most ranches, I suppose. The men aren't in them much except to sleep. Ours sit up at the house evenings until bedtime. We light a fire in the fireplace and—"

"One of them strums a guitar, I suppose?" Kevin's tone was as smooth as water sliding over rocks.

Suddenly angry, Annette turned to look at him squarely, her chin lifted. "Come to think of it, Sam does —sometimes. He knows lots of the old-time songs—the old-time ways—"

Before his lazily amused glance she stopped abruptly. Kevin shrugged. "Let him keep 'em."

Annette left him there and followed Ronnie who had reached the chicken pen. "That's our egg supply."

"Every day?"

She nodded. "Maybe you can help get them to the kitchen every day."

Kevin had come up behind them. "They ever get out?"

She shook her head. "Not lately. Something's been trying to get at them."

"What?"

"We don't know—for sure. Coyote probably. Sophie keeps a loaded gun over the kitchen door just in case she hears anything in the night."

"Guns. That's what I like," Kevin said quietly. He

turned to look up at the Big Horns. "Ever go up there?"

"Part way. I've been up to the summer pasture."

"Can we go up there while we're here?" Ronnie asked eagerly.

"We'll try to go in that direction," Annette promised. "I won't say how far." She had almost mentioned that there were good reasons to avoid the whole distance, but thought better of it.

"Is there anything you'd like to do with the rest of the day?" she asked Kevin, making her tone carefully polite. "Maybe you'd just rather loaf, then do something tomorrow."

The corners of his mouth again flicked her that ironic little smile. "Right."

Completely frustrated, Annette turned toward the house leaving him there. Immediately she heard feet running up behind her and glanced back to see Ronnie. "Can't we do *some*thing today?" he begged.

Annette smiled at him. "Let's do. Let's take a walk along the creek, then tomorrow we'll ride."

For almost a mile they followed the bank of the stream until finally they were under the cottonwoods on Nally land. Ronnie promptly stripped off his sneakers and socks and waded in, rolling the legs of his shorts as high as possible. After watching a few minutes Annette rolled up the legs of her jeans and did likewise.

"What do you boys do to entertain yourselves at home?"

"Me, I swim at the Y. Summers I belong to the

Little League. This will be more fun, though. Gee, I never had a crick before!"

"What does Kevin do with himself?" Annette asked. It might be important to know that.

Ronnie slipped on a rock, caught his balance, and stood on one foot like a crane as he examined the toe he had stubbed. "Oh—Kev—I dunno. Kev doesn't like lots of things, I guess." Ronnie's tone was vague. "He goes down to the Y and practices at the shooting range. Sometimes he plays basketball, but not very often. Last year the coach at high school tried to get him to go out for the team but he wouldn't do it."

"But why not? Most boys would love that."

By now Ronnie was trying to corner a trout in an eddy against the bank and was dodging back and forth. "Yep, they would. But not Kev!"

Annette felt disturbed by all this vague information. She was responsible for entertaining Kevin Way for a whole month, and if he didn't like anything. . . .

"But, isn't there something he likes to do—besides shoot? Does he like school?" At least that would give them something to talk about.

Ronnie gave up on the trout, cupped great handfuls of water and flung them high so they splashed down on him as he turned his face skyward to meet them. "Yeah. Kevin likes school. Reads a lot, too." He opened his eyes and frowned at Annette in an honest attempt to explain his brother. Annette understood. Explaining Kevin Way was not simple. "Thing is, Kev doesn't like having to do things just because somebody tells him to—or when they tell him."

"But how does that work in school?"

Ronnie grinned. "It doesn't. He flunked geometry last winter, almost flunked English this spring. Made Pop mad. Kev's really pretty good at both of 'em."

Annette ran a hand through her windblown dark curls. "Then why did he almost flunk?"

Ronnie scrambled up the bank and sat down to face her. "Because he waited until the last week before report cards every six weeks, then turned in to the teacher every written paper that had been assigned all at once. Usually the last day before grades closed. The teachers didn't like it."

"But—why did he do it?"

Ronnie lifted his shoulders and let them fall. "Search me! When Pop asks him, Kev says that way the teacher can get a good overall look at what he can do. Trouble is they do. When I'm in high school I hope I can write papers as well as he does. The teachers can't find a thing wrong except they're late. You know, I guess Kev's just a nut!"

Ronnie gave her a relieved bright-eyed look as though glad he had finally hit on an explanation.

"So what you mean is that Kevin does everything well but in his own good time!"

"Yep." Ronnie was pulling on his socks and sneakers. "I like you!"

Whew! I hope I never have to ask Kevin to do any-

thing! "I like you, too, Ronnie. We'd better start back. I have to help Martha with supper."

Ronnie stood. "Pop's brought Kev out here to stay on a real ranch while he finishes his book because he doesn't know what to do with him in New York."

"I hope we can fill the bill," Annette told him dryly.

"Me an' Pop hope you can, too."

Annette did not express her next thought aloud. *Good grief, and I'm stuck with that Operation Deepfreeze for a month!*

10   *Kevin's Other Side*

Sam and John came to the table that night dressed in clean work clothes and without the extras about which they had teased Sophie. Ronnie was obviously disappointed.

"Are you a cowboy?" he asked either of them who would answer.

Sam grinned. "I suppose you'd call us that—at least from time to time."

"Can I go along when you punch cows?"

"The cows are up on summer range and we don't

punch them the old way anymore. You can go if Sophie says so."

Ronnie turned his attention to John. "Are you an Indian?"

Professor Way stepped in. "Ronnie, you ask too many questions and you're embarrassing."

To everyone's surprise John took the inquisition in stride. "I'm an Arapaho."

"Gee! I know you never scalped anybody. It's too late for that—I learned in history—but did your father maybe? Was he a chief?"

Annette watched for John to freeze. Instead, he laughed. Before he could find an answer, Professor Way spoke sternly. "Ronnie, you should be scalped for asking such questions. Stop!"

Kevin's eyes lifted to John, turned to his father. "Can you blame him? Dark as that fellow is?"

John's head lifted, his fork halfway to his mouth. He laid it down, his eyes flashing, started to push back from the table. Shocked and angered, Annette felt herself half rise. Martha was sitting between Annette and John and quietly she reached out and put one hand on the knee of each of them, firmly pushing them back into their chairs.

Sophie spoke directly to Kevin, quietly firm. "John's been with us for years and his mother before him—until she passed away. She's buried in our family plot. John's with us summers, in school at the reservation the rest of the time. He has an excellent record."

"That's more'n Kevin's got," Ronnie observed.

Professor Way drew a long breath, pulled out his handkerchief and mopped his brow. "It's very hot," he observed.

Sophie took the cue. "You'll sleep under a blanket tonight."

Talk then shifted to temperatures with everyone but John and Kevin taking part. Annette made little contribution because she was thinking with regret that every time John's relations with the white man were about to level off into agreeability something upset them. She wondered if perhaps the only people he would ever get along with would be Sophie, Martha, Sam, and another Arapaho.

The meal was finally finished. Martha rose and the professor followed suit. "That was a wonderful meal, Miss Lowery."

Martha's face creased with pleasure, and she bestowed a benevolent glance on Ronnie as he came through with an enthusiastic "Sure was!" Kevin rose without comment.

"We'll have a fire now. We can sit and talk," Sophie told them.

"Thank you, Miss Lowery, but I think I'll get my notes in order for tomorrow and that we'll all go to bed early," the professor told her pleasantly. "None of us slept well last night."

When they had gone, Sophie's tone was indignant. "That Kevin! His manners are bad."

"Whatever he is, we're stuck with it for a month," Martha observed. "I guess we can put up with his manners for fifty dollars a week. You need that money for an irrigation turbine, so you won't have to do so much handwork."

Sam was getting a drink at the sink. "We'll corral him. Colts kick up their heels on the quiet side sometimes, an' maybe he's just doin' his kickin'. "

Annette debated whether to tell them the information Ronnie had given her this afternoon, but decided against it. Things would probably work out in a little time.

It took less than a week to discover how completely wrong she was.

Kevin spent the first three days occupied with a pile of paperback mysteries he had brought. In between bouts with these he took short strolls about the buildings, his manner critical, dissatisfied, and bored. One could read his state of mind. He had been brought here for a month on a ranch—against his will.

Because she had been appointed to care for the entertainment of the boys, Annette asked them every day if they wished to ride, hike, or swim. Ronnie's replies were immediate and definite. He wanted all three every day. He did not mind that she was a girl giving directions. His admiration for her was open and boundless and he told her so. Everyday and everything in it interested him—especially if she shared it.

Kevin, however, observed her with a faint lazy smile

and shook his head when she asked his wishes. Because she felt responsible, she was left seething and frustrated. "I shouldn't care—if that's the way he wants it," she kept telling herself.

The answer would probably have been sufficient had it not been that Sophie and Martha seemed to feel that because she was Kevin's age, they should like each other and she should be able to handle the problem.

"Annette, maybe Kevin would like to ride today," Sophie would suggest, a note of worry in her voice.

More often it was Martha. "Annette, are you sure Kevin has something interesting to do today? It does seem. . . ."

The only answer Annette could make, and finally she made it with some heat, was that Kevin saw nothing remotely interesting at the Circle Y.

"That's the way it is! I'm sorry." She felt her voice shake with tears. "I've tried. I can't get him to do *any-thing*."

They had both stared at her for a moment as though it would be impossible for anyone to find the Circle Y and herself uninteresting. After that, they said little, but she knew they were disturbed and she could not help feeling to blame more than before.

If Professor Way was concerned he did not show it. His typewriter tapped through the day, broken only by the rustling of paper, the communing of the author to himself. He had left his sons to Annette and the great outdoors with the idea that these should be enough for anybody. He seemed not to have noticed the fact that Kevin's idea of the outdoors was a book and the chair in the yard, and that Annette was the least of his thoughts.

Annette found Sam her main source of confidence now. "If this was a plush hotel, maybe he'd like it," she told the old man.

"Maybe we could put a desk in the kitchen for a lobby," he suggested with the lifting and falling of his heavy brows.

"Why not let him alone," John advised shortly, the first time he had addressed her since the vacuum cleaner incident.

"Because Martha and Sophie think I should entertain him. I guess he just doesn't like me."

"Consider yourself lucky," John said briefly.

John was probably right but the cousins were paying her ten dollars a week to entertain the two boys. Somehow she had to earn it. She and Ronnie, sometimes Mary, rode the trails that crisscrossed the valley and the benchland. Ronnie caught on quickly to handling Piebald and enjoyed himself thoroughly.

Once, as Annette had done before him, he pointed up to the peaks. "Why don't we follow that trail?"

Immediately Mary shook her head. "That's loaded country up there—bear, even a moose sometimes. Better stay where it's safe."

A week later Annette had proof that Mary did not follow her own advice. Ronnie went to the hayfield with the men, and Annette, catching up in the garden, looked northwest just in time to see a big brown horse pass the spring where the trails branched and entered the upper country.

"Why, that's Mary's Bullet—and Mary."

She asked to use Martha's binoculars and she studied the horse and rider. From such a great distance Annette could not see much, but Mary was carrying something behind the saddle. That afternoon, after Kevin again refused activity, Annette mounted Cindy and cut across toward the spring, thinking to ride home with her friend.

She was well beyond the spring when she saw Mary coming from above. Anticipating her friend's surprise, Annette pulled Cindy in behind an aspen clump and let Mary pass her. Behind the saddle Mary carried two saddlebags which hung as though they were empty. As Mary passed, Annette noted her moody expression.

Annette turned Cindy loose to trot down and catch up with Bullet. Mary wheeled in the saddle at the sound of hoofs, her face so frightened that Annette pulled Cindy to a halt. "Why, what's the matter?"

"Wh-what are you doing here? You've been spying on me!"

"Spying?" Annette was indignant. "I saw you ride out this morning. I came to meet you and ride home. That's all. Mary, what's wrong?"

Mary blinked, swallowed, drew a long breath as though struggling for composure. She drew her hand from her face down across her throat and the hand quivered a little. Suddenly she started Bullet on. "I'm sorry, Annette."

They rode along side by side, each wondering what to say. "Mary, is something wrong?" Annette asked finally.

"No, of course not! Why should there be? You scared me—coming up behind like that! I didn't know anyone was within miles."

"What have you been doing?" Annette asked. "Some of your cattle stray?"

Mary was herself now. "I thought so this morning, but I can see from here that there are ten down in the flat. Guess I've had my ride for nothing."

Annette, riding on Mary's left, found herself looking at the edge of a blue work shirt showing from beneath the flap of the near saddlebag. Mary noted her glance, reached down and tucked the edge in and fastened the loose strap of the bag.

I wonder where she's really been, Annette thought.

During the next few days Annette tapered off on asking Kevin his wishes. The business was tiresome and embarrassing. Martha sided with her when Sophie chided her. "That one's too lazy and he enjoys turning people down, disapproving of things. Let him sit!"

Although Martha usually followed Sophie's thinking, she was occasionally solid in her own decision, and then Sophie did not argue. Annette still felt troubled about Kevin, especially when he began showing signs of restlessness. It was Ronnie, however, who finally pitched

Kevin's performance in a direction that kept them all busy.

At the breakfast table he stirred Kevin up with a verbal stick. "Bet I can ride better'n you can now."

Kevin eyed his brother cynically. "Huh!"

"Bet you!" Ronnie goaded.

"Listen, twerp! I can outride you any day of the week!"

"Prove it!" Ronnie yelped at him.

"Okay! This afternoon."

Sophie seized the situation as though it were an answer to all problems. "You young folks better ride this morning while it's cool."

Annette hurried through the kitchen work, pulled on her riding clothes, and headed for the corrals just in time to hear Ronnie's furious wail. "Why didn't you shut the gate?"

Then she saw four horses tear out the open gate into the unfenced grazing land, their tails aloft, hoofs flashing. Ronnie wheeled to her. "He came in and didn't shut the gate!"

Kevin gave a little shrug. "Sorry!" He sauntered away, leaving Ronnie and Annette to head the escaped culprits back to the corral, a job that took the rest of the morning.

"Let's ride today," Kevin suggested the next morning.

"At two o'clock," Annette told him firmly.

She saddled the horses and tied them before he came.

Kevin went directly to White-Eye, who stood with his head drooped, his eyes half closed. "Doesn't look like he's got much on the ball."

Annette swallowed her irritation. "Have you neck-reined?"

He swung easily into the saddle and rode down the lane without waiting for her or Ronnie. Annette trotted up beside him. "We'll ride down to Nallys. I want you to meet Mary."

They found her in the corral trying to get a bottle of milk down an orphaned lamb. Her expression was a mixture of welcome and shyness. "His mama will have none of him. I'm trying to pull him through."

As Annette introduced Kevin she was surprised at his expression, the open friendly smile that transformed his whole face as he looked over the fence at the pair. "So Mary had a little lamb," he quoted.

Mary laughed. "For now anyhow. I wish he'd get on his feet. This is a three times a day performance."

Kevin tied his horse. Inside the corral he bent and lifted the lamb gently to all fours, held it so until it braced wobbly legs and stood swaying. "There he is—on his feet." He spread his hands proudly.

Mary stared at him with her mouth open. "But—I did that. He just folded up again. Now you come along. . . ."

The lamb took a tentative step, made a murmuring bleat. Kevin spread his hands facetiously. "Just shows to go you! He probably was ready, as of this moment,

ANNETTE

to get up anyhow. Knows his own mind. That's all. I like things that know their own minds."

Annette could only look at the two of them and marvel. Something about Mary had brought out the best in Kevin, whether it was genuine or not. In the next few minutes he asked questions about the ranch and, of more significance, listened to the answers.

Annette's thoughts combined puzzlement and relief. "He never asked any of us such questions and wouldn't have listened if we'd told him. He likes her. That's it. The rest of us have been forced on him, so he can ignore us."

Her relief came from the feeling that if Kevin liked something or somebody things might be better. "Do you have time for a ride?" she asked Mary.

Mary debated, shook her head. "I'd better not. Mother isn't feeling well. I've made her stay in bed."

Kevin looked disappointed. "Better luck next time," he told her. "We'll try again."

As they rode away, Annette had a feeling that Mary would have liked to accompany them. She glanced back and waved, and saw that the girl was looking after them wistfully.

"We'll have time for a ride up on the bench," she told the boys as she turned Cindy into a tramped trail that bordered the edge of the Nally hayfield. "Get in single file behind me along here."

Kevin's expression had returned to its old rebellion. "Why do we have to keep the nags off this grass stuff?"

"There'll be a second hay cutting for the Nallys. They need it."

"As though three horses would hurt it!"

He dropped back, however, until the hay area ended and they were climbing up the benchland. Suddenly Kevin kicked White-Eye into a startled lope, passed Ronnie and Annette and went flying on up the slope at full speed, pounding the horse's ribs with his heels. When Cindy and Piebald caught up, Kevin was face down beside the spring, drinking.

"You really do ride," she told Kevin. "How come you haven't wanted to ride before this?"

He sat up, wiping water from his face. "Sure, I've ridden. It's nothing new!"

11 *Chicken Thief*

While Ronnie and Annette were drinking, Kevin mounted, let out a sudden exuberant yell and went flying up the steep trail beyond the spring with the horse plunging and scrambling dangerously. Annette swung to Cindy's saddle. White-Eye was both frightened and angry, his tail switching, his eyes rolling. Then he bucked, and she held her breath. Kevin's arm raised and he slapped the horse across the rump. They went flying on and up.

Annette pulled Cindy up. "Kevin! Stop!"

148

Either he did not hear or did not care to hear. White-Eye dashed on, his muscles corded. Rocks rolled. Annette turned and shouted back at Ronnie. "I'm cutting across to the trail coming down the other side of the rocks. Go back, Ronnie!"

Then she galloped Cindy along a quarter-mile stretch of grass to meet Kevin. "I've got to stop him!"

She reached the down trail within minutes and just in time to hear White-Eye's sliding hoofs on the shale. Then they came galloping into sight. The horse slipped on a wet place and skidded dangerously close to the rampart that dropped to the benchland below. Wet with sweat he came on. Annette swung Cindy sideways in the wide trail, and for a moment she thought White-Eye would plunge into Cindy. At the last minute he slid to a stop.

Kevin grinned teasingly and tried to pass, but Annette caught White-Eye's rein. For a moment she and Kevin were knee to knee as the horses danced on the trail. "Stop it! Walk your horse!"

"Couldn't you keep up?" Kevin grinned.

"Sophie'll flay you alive for abusing her horse. Walk him the rest of the way in."

White-Eye was tossing his head, and she released the rein and moved out in front of him. The gelding, however, had had enough. Sophie had said he was a gentleman as long as he was well treated. The rules had been broken. He reared and plunged into Cindy, then went into a bucking fit on an eight-foot ledge.

Annette saw Kevin go off the far side and roll towards the edge as White-Eye dashed away down the trail. Kevin's arm clutched a rock projection as he slipped over, and he held on. Annette was off Cindy and pulling on him desperately as the rock started to give. Ronnie came up, and together they hauled Kevin back up.

White beneath his tan, he gave them a shaky but droll grin. "Darn him! He almost did me in!"

Annette opened her mouth to say something scathing, but could think of nothing adequate. "You bring him in, Ronnie." She mounted and left them there.

White-Eye, still damp with sweat and angry, was grazing two miles below. He had stepped on a trailing rein and snapped it off. He flattened his ears as she moved up to reach for it, then abandoned the idea of a fight as she spoke soothingly. As they moved toward home, Annette saw Ronnie coming half a mile behind. Kevin's head showed a hundred yards behind him above the sage.

"I hope he's worn out when he gets in!"

Sophie's eyes widened as she saw White-Eye. As Annette began to explain she felt a sudden letdown and stopped talking as she knew sobs were coming.

"You did exactly right, Annette," Sophie assured her. "Rub him down, and don't give him any water for an hour. He's still mad. Don't let him nip you."

From the kitchen fifteen minutes later Annette saw Sophie talking to Professor Way, her head bobbing indignantly, while Kevin sat in the yard chair looking at a magazine and ignoring both of them.

Professor Way's voice rose. "Kevin and I will discuss this. It will not happen again."

From then on, Kevin reverted to his original attitude —indifference.

By now Sophie's poultry flock had dwindled to a dozen hens, roosting high in a tight little group for protection. Despite a wire fence, hens kept going in the middle of the night, sometimes with loud squawks, sometimes without a cackle.

"Sophie, are you sure it isn't some*one*?" Annette asked.

Sophie glanced at her. "Forget the Nally business. The sheriff says he's no longer in the vicinity. Besides, there are coyote tracks out there."

Kevin glanced at the old shotgun over the kitchen door. "Why don't you set somebody guard with that shotgun at night?"

Sophie smiled amiably. "It's easier to go out of the chicken business. Not much profit in it anyhow."

Kevin was usually the first to break the fire circle evenings, but tonight he was the last to leave the kitchen. He had been good-humored, smiling a little at Sam's jokes, teasing Ronnie now and then. They left him there staring at the dying fire.

Sometime during the night the roar of the old shotgun brought everybody out. As Annette, pulling on her bathrobe and following Sophie's flopping old slippers, came out she saw Sam and John coming from the bunkhouse. Then she saw Kevin standing near the chicken pen, the old shotgun in his hand.

He turned toward Sophie. "I think I got him!"

Sophie pulled her look away from him, opened the wire gate of the chicken yard and walked in. Sam followed, throwing ahead of her the beam of a flashlight.

Kevin was right. On the floor inside the small building lay a dead coyote, and around him and on top of him was what was left of the Lowery poultry flock. The old scatter-gun had gotten them all.

"For—heaven's sake!" Sophie's voice sounded weak as though it came from a distance. John ran a slow hand through his tousled black hair and said nothing. Annette felt as though she had been stricken dumb.

It was Sam who found his voice. He turned to Kevin with something as close to violence as the old man could muster. "Now what in tarnation did you do that for?"

"Somebody needed to do something about that coyote," Kevin told him firmly. "I did it!"

Sophie broke her dumbfounded silence. "But, suppose it hadn't been a coyote? Once we thought maybe a thief—"

Kevin shrugged as he turned toward the house. "If it was a man he had no business there. He'd have deserved what he got."

"Well, I suppose we may as well leave this mess till morning," John said.

"No, we won't," Martha said firmly. "He's put us

out of the chicken business, but those hens were cleanly shot, and we'll dress them."

"You mean—tonight?" Annette asked feebly.

Martha stepped in and began gathering up the hens, and the two men followed suit. Sophie had already headed for the kitchen, and stove lids began rattling. Kevin came out and headed for the guesthouse. The professor and Ronnie had slept through it all.

It was a night Annette would not forget the rest of her life. At two o'clock she looked around and wanted to laugh. The women, bathrobes pulled over their night-clothes, were still pulling stubborn pinfeathers and dressing the chickens as fast as the men scalded and plucked them. Boiling water made the kitchen steamy. They worked fast and silently. Loose feathers had settled all over the room.

Finally the twelve hens lay cooling on trays in the refrigerator. The dying teakettle hissed softly as they all sat down. "What you going to do with that kid?" Sam asked.

"I guess I'll have to talk to his father in the morning." Sophie's tone was uncertain.

"What good'll that do?" John asked. "Come daylight, there's three men I'd load into the station wagon and dump at the first bus stop."

Martha firmly set him straight. "We been paid in advance to take these people for a month. Six hundred dollars."

Sophie added to the reasoning. "We promised food,

lodging, and entertainment. We have to come through on that."

Annette concealed a smile. How like Martha to be thinking of cash and Sophie of the promises made and to be kept.

Sam shrugged. "He sure had his entertainment tonight. Come on, John. It's way past bedtime." Their expressions indicated that what Kevin Way needed was a man's firm hand. Annette conceded that they might be right.

In the morning Sophie was firm. "Professor, last night Kevin took my shotgun and killed every hen I had left."

The professor's eyes blinked. "He did? Why?"

Kevin spoke defensively. "A coyote had been killing the hens."

"I have no desire to have anyone shot on my premises," Sophie continued, "and that could have happened. I want Kevin's promise that he will not touch a gun again so long as he is here."

The professor turned to his son. "Promise that, Kevin."

Kevin hesitated sulkily. "Okay."

Later she saw the two arguing outside the guesthouse, the professor gesturing, Kevin protesting. The words came in snatches. "Ronnie seems to be—can't you?—besides just sit around! Keep out—people's hair —enough for me to finish this book!" The guesthouse door slammed shut.

Later Kevin sought out Annette. "Riding today?" His manner was diffident for a change, a little embarrassed.

"I have to take fresh water to the men in the hayfield. Ronnie's going, maybe Mary."

Annette put Kevin's saddle on Piebald early. White-Eye would probably pitch him over the fence. Kevin made no comment when his brother proudly climbed on the big horse while he was relegated to the smaller one. On the way to Nallys, White-Eye flattened his ears every time Kevin came close.

Mary greeted them with enthusiasm. "Mother's up today and I feel like riding." When they had picked up the water jug back at the ranch, Ronnie and Annette rode ahead and Kevin stayed beside Mary. Again Annette felt grateful for this girl's effect on him.

At the hayfield, Sam teased the three of them but ignored Kevin. He seemed undisturbed by the obvious rebuff and walked off by himself to examine the stacker and then watched it work when the men started up after their rest.

"I think I'll come help with this in the morning," he told Annette. "I like that machine."

Won't the men love that! Annette thought.

The afternoon was comfortable and fun, for Kevin was a good entertainer when he chose to be. He was also completely agreeable. Annette's watch had stopped, and when she gasped and said she must hurry home to help Martha, Kevin made a suggestion.

"I'll take Mary home and bring in the cows on the way back."

Annette was taken by surprise that he had ever noticed that there were cows to be brought in.

In the morning, Kevin came to breakfast with his father and the family. "Imagine seeing you up at six o'clock in the morning," Martha observed.

He grinned at her. "Think I'll help with the hay."

"That'll be work," Sam remarked dryly.

"Just don't be late for supper," Martha added.

"What are we going to have?" he asked.

"Chicken," she answered quietly. The rest of the meal was eaten in silence.

Annette felt a sense of relief as Kevin climbed into the jeep with Sam and John, both a little stiff-backed and disapproving. This would relieve her of responsibility for Kevin for one day.

"Sam and John would have wriggled out of that if they could," she told Martha.

"No doubt," her cousin replied briefly. "So would I. The Ways are paying for this summer though, so we'll try to see they get their money's worth. So far the professor has paid the damages."

Neither Professor Way nor the Lowery sisters had any idea how expensive the damages might have been before this day was out had it not been for quick work on the part of Sam, John, and Annette. Annette was part of the scene only because Sophie had sent her to the hayfield with a large sheet of folded canvas behind her saddle.

"Today's the last day of haying, and I think I'll have one stack of hay to sell. I want to keep it in good shape. Sam couldn't find this sheet this morning."

Annette rode Cindy to the field. When she arrived, the men were just piling the last load of hay onto the top of a haystack with the loader. Annette could see why Sophie was pleased. For the last two miles, as she had headed south, she had passed a haystack every quarter of a mile. They reminded her of humped sentinels down the valley.

Kevin was helping, after a fashion, picking up hay with a fork and tossing it up on top of the stack. The south breeze kept blowing it back.

John was up on top of the stack pushing the forkfuls of hay about to shape up the stack. "Never mind the rest of it down there," he called down to Kevin. "There's a lot of weed in it anyhow."

Kevin immediately desisted. As Annette rode up she saw him do something she had not seen before. He pulled a package of cigarettes from his shirt pocket and lit one. Carelessly he tossed the match away. It landed, still burning, in the side of the haystack.

Annette screamed. "Kevin, put out that match. Hurry!"

Kevin wheeled to give her a puzzled look, not even aware of what he had done. John had already slid off the far side of the haystack with Sam. The two came rushing around the end of the pile as the match caught the hay and flamed high.

John yelled, snatched up a fork, and plunged it deep into the stack above the burning hay, bringing out the flame and dropping it on the ground. Against the wind, the stubble caught fire even as the two men leaped in and tried to trample it down. Annette leaped from Cindy and began stepping on wisps of flames that were escaping in every direction.

Kevin had backed away, staring with his mouth open at the thing he had caused. Annette shouted at him. "Get in here! Do something!"

Belatedly he began trampling flames, but the wind was too high. It was carrying the flame away from the stack, but also down the valley toward all the other waiting stacks. Sophie's whole winter feed crop would go up in flames.

Then Sam shouted at her. "Get that canvas! Hurry!"

She rushed at Cindy, standing with dropped reins, frightening the little mare so that she dodged away. Annette slowed, spoke soothingly, and caught her. Kevin had dashed to her other side now, was untying the saddle strings that held the canvas. Together they hauled it to the creeping flames, slapped it down with the fire leaping almost around them. Smoke rolled from beneath the cloth as they smothered the fire, hauling the canvas back and forth across the yards of burning stubble.

The canvas was heavy. It took the strength of all four

of them to pull it across the fire, which seemed always to burst out in new spots as soon as the wind got at it again. Smoke choked them, blackened their hands and faces.

"Get—the jeep—out of the way," John ordered Annette, his speech breaking up into fits of coughing as he worked. "It'll burn, too, if—you—don't."

Annette got the jeep a hundred yards away, rushed back to help with the fire, able to see at this distance that Kevin was fighting with the rest of them. Cindy had taken to her heels and was gone.

Ten minutes later they had won. They stood to one side gasping for air, drawing in great breaths. Sam took out his bandanna and mopped his brow. Shaking, he sat down on the ground and dropped his head on his knees.

"You all right?" John asked.

Sam nodded without raising his head. John was blackened with smoke, and both he and Annette had small burns on their arms. Their clothes were scorched and dirty. He stood looking down at Sam until he was sure the old man was all right. Then he turned toward Kevin, standing off to one side.

"You!" he said low and bitterly. "Are you crazy? Pitching a lighted match into a haystack of all things!"

Kevin watched him and stammered. "I—I didn't know that's where the match lit. I didn't mean—"

The words were cut short, for John pitched himself at Kevin with a fury that took them both to the ground.

Kevin grunted when he hit, and then the two were rolling over and over, pummeling and striking.

Annette screamed. Sam jumped to his feet and ran
to them. He tried to push them apart without success.
As they rolled against him, almost knocking him off his
feet, he grabbed a head of hair in each hand and pulled
until they fell away from each other, panting and staring
up at him.

"Now, you two young cubs, get on your feet and
behave yourselves," he snapped. "What makes you think
you have to fight?" he asked John.

"He was about to burn the haystack!" gritted John.
"He wouldn't have even cared."

"Mebbe not," Sam agreed, "but let Sophie Lowery
settle it her own way since that's what she's goin' to do
anyhow. Now get for home, both of you."

Annette and Sam got into the jeep and headed for
the house. They came to the two boys, one walking a
hundred feet ahead of the other. Sam passed Kevin without inviting him to ride, then he picked up John. His
eyes still burned, and his face held more hatred than
Annette had ever seen.

"Hadn't we better—" Annette began as he gunned
the motor and started on.

"No!" Sam told her explosively.

Before they reached the house they found Sophie coming back on Cindy. She sighed as they reported what
had happened. "It's a good thing the haying's done. Now
we can all keep an eye on Kevin."

"Huh!" Sam snorted. "The hull five of us couldn't keep that one in check."

For the next three days things were very quiet around the Circle Y. The unique thing about the next misfortune was that Kevin was not the cause of it and that he briefly became more of a help than a hindrance.

Mary Nally came riding into the yard late one afternoon. She walked into the house without waiting to knock. Her face was worried, her eyes wide with fear. Annette and Martha were alone in the kitchen.

"Miss Lowery—could you come and help me? I— Mother's terribly sick, and there isn't anything more I can do for her!"

She dropped her face in her hands suddenly and wept.

12 *Pack Trip*

Annette saw a new side to Martha then. The reserved silent woman who, by choice, confined herself to yard and kitchen, put her lean arms around the girl and held her so for a long moment. "Just cry a minute. Annette, get my medicine satchel from the closet shelf in my bedroom. Somebody get the car out."

When the Lowery sisters, Mary, and Annette got into the station wagon John had brought to the yard gate and left with the motor running, they found Kevin in the back seat. Martha's lips parted as though to order him out. Then she settled wordlessly beside Sophie, who headed for the Nally ranch at a pace that made Annette wonder if the old station wagon was about to leave its gears and glass scattered over the Wyoming countryside.

Annette and Kevin waited in the kitchen while the sisters and Mary went to the bedroom. Annette could hear the dry hacking cough inside the room and she could hear Martha's quiet voice, its usual harshness softened to quiet firm authority as she asked questions.

Moments later they all returned to the kitchen and Martha stood beside the window studying the thermometer. She turned. "Sophie, drive to Stone Gulch and bring back Dr. Blase."

As Sophie started out, Martha followed her to the door. "Don't scatter his bones all over the county either! I need him."

Sophie went meekly, the rest waited for an hour and a half. Mary paced back and forth across the room, her eyes wide with worry. Kevin rose and gently pushed her down into the chair he had been using. His concern for someone beside himself left everyone blinking.

Martha tried to busy herself in the kitchen. "Mary, how long has your mother had this cough?"

"Since March, when she caught that heavy cold. She couldn't seem to shake it."

"Doesn't weigh what she used to either, does she?" Martha pursued.

"I think she must have lost at least twenty pounds."

Everyone stirred with relief when Sophie tore back

into the yard and ushered into the house a graying stout man still hanging to his hat and his dignity as though he had been recently threatened with the loss of both.

From the kitchen Annette could hear him for the next half hour asking questions. When finally he and Martha returned to the kitchen, his voice was hearty and encouraging but fooled no one. "I'll have some tests run on these slides I've taken, and by tomorrow I'll have answers. Meanwhile, keep her down and warm, and let her rest."

Martha stayed at the Nally home that night. When the others at the Circle Y were settled around the fire, Kevin was obviously restless, but it was a restlessness without his usual ironic irritability. At noon the next day he asked Sophie a question. "Okay if I go down to Nallys'?"

Sophie looked at him doubtfully and he cleared the hurdle she was obviously building ahead of her. "I just want to know the news, maybe sit around with Mary if she isn't busy—or see if she needs anything."

"I suppose so," Sophie said doubtfully. "But—"

"I know." He gave her a grin with a hint of shame in it. "Behave myself."

Sophie smiled at him. Kevin at his best could be charming. After he had gone she seemed worried. "I wonder if I should have let him go."

He returned barely in time for supper, his usually neat clothes rumpled, bits of hay clinging to his hair and shoulders, his hands and face smudged and grimy.

"Mrs. Nally's got tuberculosis. The doctor says she'll have to go to a sanatorium."

"Oh, dear!" exclaimed Sophie. "How are the Nallys going to manage that?"

"The doc seems to have it managed," he told her. "Martha said to tell you an ambulance would take Mrs. Nally down to the sanatorium at Greybull in the morning, and that she'd go along and come back on the bus. The doc says Mrs. Nally's got a good chance if they get things started right away."

"How did Mary take it?" Sophie asked as they sat down to supper.

"She was pretty upset. I did what I could—milked the cow, drove the sheep in, carried water."

"*You* milked the cow?" Sophie's tone was a feeble squeak.

Kevin chuckled. "The cow didn't think much of it, and my hands hurt, but we got by."

Professor Way looked pleased. The rest were too dumbfounded to do more than look astonished.

Sophie recovered first. "Anything said about what Mary will do?"

"Martha tried to get her to come here, but she says she's going to stay there by herself and look after the place."

"She will not!" Sophie said flatly.

Mary, however, proved adamant. "There's the stock to be cared for, the house to be looked after."

"Now, Mary," Sophie argued, having already fore-
seen the objections, "put the cattle and sheep in with
ours. Bring Bullet along and lock the house. We want
you."

"Please!" Annette pleaded.

"Please," Kevin urged.

"Aw, come on!" Ronnie exploded.

Mary remained firm. She would stay and look after
Nally interests herself.

Two nights later, however, the group was just breaking up around the fire when the sound of a galloping
horse reached their ears. The sound became louder,
then stopped at the gate. Sophie turned on the yard
light and they all saw Mary Nally loop the reins over
a post and come hurrying toward the house. Unexpectedly, she slowed to a leisurely pace, and as she
entered she cast a nervous smile at all of them.

"I decided to take your offer and stay down here,"
she said.

"In the middle of the night?" Ronnie exclaimed.

Everybody laughed, but all eyes were on Mary. She
was without an overnight bag and dressed in jeans and
a work-rumpled blouse. Mary's eyes briefly met Annette's
with a certain glassy brightness.

"I—I guess I just got scared," she explained. "I just
left."

"I'm glad," Annette told her. "You can share my
room."

"We're all glad," Sophie welcomed her. "We worried

about you down there alone."

"I'll put your horse away," John said quietly and went out. Sam wordlessly followed him. The Ways said good night and started for the guesthouse. As Annette pushed Mary ahead of her toward the bedroom she saw Sophie and Martha exchange a puzzled look.

She tossed pajamas on the bed where Mary had sat down with a deep tremulous sort of sigh. "What happened to scare you, Mary?"

Mary turned to look at her. "Nothing. I decided that you folks were right—and I didn't really want to stay alone. I guess, though, it does seem funny—my coming here at night this way."

"We'll all sleep better because you *are* here. Sophie and Martha have fussed about it every day. I'll go get us a pitcher of milk."

In the kitchen John was talking to Sophie in a low tone. "—halter on that horse—no bridle or saddle."

Sophie's lower lip thrust outward as she thought. "I wonder. . . ."

"Me, too," John said as he left for the night.

Mary was just slipping into the pajama tops as Annette returned to the bedroom with glasses and the pitcher of milk. Annette was startled to see three marks on the underside of Mary's upraised arm, marks that looked like finger marks turning to bruises.

I wonder what happened, Annette thought.

Mary slept late the next morning and came to the kitchen apologizing, but when her scant amount of livestock had been pastured at Circle Y, she relaxed completely, her reserve dropping away, a new warmth coming from her.

It was a time of relaxation for everybody. The haying was done and the men tended to odd tasks around the place. Kevin changed in the daily presence of this girl he admired although she seemed not to notice his special attentions. There was much laughter at the Circle Y that week. Annette felt pleased with herself because she had put away almost seventy dollars from her summer's work. Uncle Archie was going to be astonished.

In the midst of this lull, Kevin made a request. "Could we go up into the mountains before we have to go back to New York? Maybe have a pack trip?"

"I'll have to think about it," Sophie said slowly. Later, in the presence of everybody but the Ways, she thought aloud. "I'd like to go myself. I've never seen the Medicine Wheel."

Sam's eyes glowed. "There's a great campin' place right under the brow of Medicine Mountain where I used to take folks. We could borry equipment—pack-saddles, panniers, bedrolls, and such."

Characteristically Sophie made the decision. "Let's go. I'd like such a trip. See what you can get together, Sam."

Activity at Circle Y went into high gear. Sam and John began collecting equipment. Sophie sold the extra haystacks and bought two small tents. Mary was not content to leave until she had talked to the doctor at the sanatorium and had been assured that her mother was holding her own. Kevin and Ronnie went to town and bought Western riding clothes and boots. Kevin, having started this excursion, was delighted to help everybody although Sam preferred to do without him and John froze if he even came near. The men trained the big Percheron draft team to carry the packsaddles and panniers. Of them all, only the professor and Martha refused to go.

"I want to finish my work," Professor Way insisted.

"I want my feet in my own kitchen and not on a mountain," Martha told them.

The line of riders strung out shortly after daybreak of the fourth day with Sam in the lead, and immediately after he had given the group stern orders. "Now you all do what I tell you and no back talk."

As Sam had told them, progress was slow, no more than twenty miles a day with one overnight camp on the way. He kept them mostly to mountain pastures, but to save time he took them over the great rampart by a steep deer trail that seemed more adequate for the sticking qualities of flies than of horses. Sometimes the group was terrified at the heights the horses were expected to scale, but Sam took them through. There were the great peaks coming closer, the bands of sheep in the high country, the freedom, the view. Only once did Annette have a sudden shattering doubt. As the round top of Medicine Mountain loomed closer, she had a sudden feeling of wanting to turn and run back home.

"I'm crazy!" she thought. "I wanted this trip all summer. It must be just what happened up there in June."

By noon the next day they had established a base camp under trees on a long gentle slope at the top of a mountain park where there was grazing for the horses. The trees backed up against several great boulders and from around one of them there gushed a stream. The view above and below was marvelous, with the round top of Medicine Mountain now less than a mile away.

Sam had everyone at work as soon as they had dismounted and flexed the kinks from their legs. "Put White-Eye on a picket rope," he had told John, "and hobbles on the rest. They'll stay around. Everybody pull your own saddles and hang 'em over those low limbs. I'll build us a fire spot between these stones under that outcrop lip of boulder so it'll keep the rain off us—if it rains. Kevin, you an' Ronnie start getting firewood. You gals can put up the tents and stow the gear."

The tasks kept them all busy for more than an hour. By the end of that time Sam had coffee boiling, and they all rested, made sandwiches, and had a late lunch.

Annette pointed up toward Medicine Mountain. "That's where the Medicine Wheel is," she told Mary.

"What's the Medicine Wheel?" Kevin asked. He was lounging beside the fire finishing a sandwich.

Abruptly Annette hesitated. She glanced at John, sensing that perhaps he would not want this site of his people discussed. She wished she had not started the subject.

"Well, what is it?" Kevin persisted.

To Annette's relief, Sophie took over. "It's a historical spot in this region, known very little really even to people who live around here." She went on to tell of its supposedly druidic origin, what the historians and geologists said about it. "People, Indian and white, tell of having seen an occasional pygmy man in the region around the Wheel."

Kevin sat up, staring at her. "You mean lately? And you mean you believe that stuff?"

Sophie laughed and Sam grinned. "I'm reporting what's been said," Sophie replied. "This kind of country brings out tales and myths by the score, and somewhere along the way tales and myths usually go back to facts, you know."

Kevin laughed sharply. "I think that's crazy!"

Sam scowled. "Got any manners, kid? Use 'em!"

"Sorry, Sophie," Kevin said carelessly as he got to his feet. "Let's go see this relic. I wouldn't want to miss any little bitty guys running around loose."

Annette, Mary, and Ronnie rose and followed Kevin at Sophie's nod. Annette glanced behind when they were a few yards from camp and saw, to her surprise, that John was coming, too.

In half an hour they had climbed the trail and were standing on the windy round peak of Medicine Mountain. She was seeing again the great oval of stones with the seats inside and the spokes radiating out to the rim. Or was this a representation of the sun, which those ancient people had worshiped? Over the thousands of years the lines of stones had sunk farther and farther into the ground so that they looked like paths barely visible above the surface.

Kevin was looking about. "Is this all there is to it? A few lines of stones buried in the grass?"

"What did you expect after thousands of years?" Mary asked him.

Kevin shrugged. "Wouldn't know." Carelessly he bent over one of the lines, picked up a fist-sized rock and hurled it far out and down the mountain.

"Quit that!" John snapped.

Kevin turned. "Says who?"

"I do. So does Uncle Sam. See those signs?" He pointed to several stakes that Annette had not noticed before, and which carried lettered signs, DO NOT DISTURB OR DESTROY. She also noticed that John's eyes snapped dangerously. Mary spoke before she could.

"Come on, Kev. Quit it. No use spoiling things. Let's look around."

For a few minutes they wandered about studying the Wheel. Kevin, prevented from doing as he pleased about rock throwing, had lost interest and was a little angry at Mary. Soon they saw him heading back toward camp with Ronnie at his heels.

Annette and Mary left the Wheel and strolled along the west rim of the mountain and began looking down

the steep side of it into a series of broken lava formations that were almost like a jungle-gym arrangement.
Wind and weather had eroded the rock into a series
of wind holes running from a few feet to a few yards
back into the mountain and down perhaps fifty feet to a
floor that opened through the side of the mountain onto
a ledge.

John dropped down into the first of the holes and,
gripping the thin post of rock that separated it from the
next one below, dropped on down from one uneven
ledge to the next. "Used to do this when I was a kid,"
he remarked. He moved out of sight.

"Ooh, listen!" Mary exclaimed.

The wind had risen suddenly and a series of sounds
seemed to move up and down through the rock formations. The wind lessened and the sound reduced to a
thin, shrill, harplike sound that was very penetrating.

"It makes me want to turn and run," Annette shuddered.

"John, did you do that?" Mary shouted.

He peered out of a hole. "Do what?"

"Was that you or the wind?"

"Won't tell you," he retorted.

Mary shuddered and giggled simultaneously. "Let's
get out of here!"

They found a sheltered spot behind a boulder on the
edge of the Wheel and sat down out of the wind. John
went to stand beside the Wheel, arms straight at his
sides, his gaze on the center seat of stones.

He could be praying—the way he did before, Annette thought.

"This place—it's strange!" Mary said suddenly.

Annette nodded. "A person doesn't know how to say it, but so much has probably happened here in the past, it makes you feel part of it, yet frightened. I like it, though, and I'm glad I'm here."

"I'm glad of lots of things lately," Mary mused. "Glad something's being done about Mom, glad there have been people to help me, and—"

"—and glad about Kevin, I suppose?" Annette teased.

Mary took the question seriously. "I suppose any girl is glad when a boy likes her—though Kevin isn't exactly what I was looking for. I mean—he's a constantly troublesome kind of person."

"That's putting it mildly," Annette replied.

Kevin was already out of Mary's thoughts. "I'm glad of something else. I suppose you guessed that I made trips up here to bring supplies to my brother?"

"I guessed. I wondered why you took the risk with your mother sick."

"That was why. If I didn't take them, he came to the ranch. He'd grab up food, anything, and he'd try to make Mom sell the ranch and give him the money so he could get away. To get out of the mountains, he'd have to go through towns and he needed money for transportation. I could see Mom getting worse with the worry of it, and I didn't know what to do. If I talked of telling the police Mother'd get so upset I'd have to play it her way and leave supplies up beyond the spring so he'd stay away from the ranch. He enjoys having control over people and he really had Mom in his clutches."

Mary paused and let out a deep breath. "Then he came down and pestered her again. I fought with him and he slapped me. She agreed to sell the ranch and give him the money, but the next day she was sick and I came for help. Awful as it is to say it, I was glad when she got taken to the sanatorium, because then he couldn't get to her anymore. She could maybe get over TB, but she couldn't get past Tom. I'd thought I'd stay and look out for the ranch but two nights after she left he was back, hunting for food, any cash she might have left, and ammunition for a rifle he said he had."

"I wonder if that would be the rifle Sam lost up at the line cabin," Annette said.

"Could be. Then he tried to make me promise to get Mom to sign papers to sell the ranch. When I refused, we had a battle right in the kitchen, but I broke away from him and ran out into the dark. I shouted back if he didn't leave I'd call the police. He came after me, but I hid in the sage. He ransacked the house then, came out and shouted that he was leaving for good and not to tell the police. He said he was leaving the country."

"Do you think he has?"

Mary nodded. "There's nothing at the ranch to do him any good now, not even Mom or me. He's gone."

John had strolled up and was listening. Mary did not seem to mind. John probably knew the facts anyhow.

"It was almost funny when he passed a dozen feet from where I was hiding behind a sage root. He'd have killed me if he'd found me. Tom was always strange—bold, bragging, superstitious."

John looked surprised. "Tom Nally? Superstitious?"

"Now what will you do this fall?" Annette asked.

Mary sighed. "I don't know. Since I've been with you folks I've just rested and enjoyed life. I know I've got to make a plan though, and maybe I'll try to get a job in Greybull close to Mom."

During the brief pause that followed John spoke. "You like my mountain?" He was more relaxed and pleasant than Annette had ever seen him.

Annette nodded and asked a question. "John, do your people still come to the Wheel—for religious ceremonies?"

His black-eyed glance flicked her and for a moment she thought he would not reply, but he did when he saw neither scorn nor laughter in her face. "Not exactly. Some of us come every year, sometimes several times, but mostly because it's a place that has a connection with us and the past. It's hard to explain. We pray if we want to—and most of us do. It's religious in a way even though most of us are trained in the mission schools now. Coming here does something—makes us feel something—"

"It's as though somebody or something was all around," Annette supplied and was surprised at the gratitude in his face. "What do you think of the pygmy race Sophie mentioned?"

"I only know what Indians and whites both say about it, that they've been seen—the little people. I believe it." He stalked on ahead, casting the next remark back. "I only know I won't have that twerp from New York throwing rocks and spoiling things."

Camp that night was gay and noisy. They sang songs, and Sam retold his stories with all drawn close to the fire with blankets across their shoulders to cut the wind from the rear. Finally they rose, heated on one side, chilly on the other, sleepy enough for bed. For a brief period from inside the tent Annette watched Sam banking the coals to hold until morning so that they showed only a faint glow. She smiled to herself. The old man was having the time of his life. This trip was something he had never dreamed he'd be doing again. Belatedly, she realized that this was why Sophie, who usually gave the orders, was letting Sam be the boss. His pleasure would not have been so complete if anyone else had given them.

"I love it, too," she thought. "I hated coming to Wyoming this summer. I was mad at Uncle Archie but now I'm glad about the whole thing. When we get back to the ranch I'll write Aunt Lila and Uncle Archie more often."

Then her eyelids closed, and the flame winked out

entirely, and so did the night sounds, the clumping of the horses' hobbled feet, the cries of night birds, the distant howling of some wild creature, the muttering of a big owl. She knew nothing more until Sam's hail roused them to help with breakfast.

Annette never forgot the next two days. Sam put John in charge of the hikes because John knew the country. "An' ifen he says don't do somethin', thet's what he means," he growled at them.

One day they walked to a lake several miles away, and the second day they followed a meandering trail up to a glacier. Often they just sat talking, or even just looking. Sometimes they climbed rocks, but only when John said that it was all right, except once when Kevin, without warning, began scrambling up the side of a long sloping cliff with tons of rubble above it.

"Come down," John told him shortly. "That stuff could slip and bury you."

Kevin went ahead as if he had not heard. A few trickles of rubble began cascading down. "I said come back!" John said authoritatively.

Then as Kevin caught his footing and went on up, John went after him with great leaps, caught him by the arm, spun him about and sent him sliding back down. As an avalanche of small rock and shale let loose from above, John came down in leaps ahead of it, hauled Kevin to his feet, and flung himself and the boy out of the path of the cascade. All of them fled then, but looking back Annette could see that the whole area where the five of them had been standing was covered with rock a yard deep. Kevin nevertheless flung himself away from John, his eyes blazing, his jaw set. "Get away from me!" he yelled.

"Kevin, shut up and behave yourself!" Mary cried. "John's in charge."

"Not of me!" Kevin stepped out of the path away from John and fell in behind the others as they walked ahead. John was now striding ahead as though none of this concerned him. Annette could see, in a way, why Kevin objected to orders from John. The Indian was two years younger despite his greater size.

"What's wrong with Kevin?" Sophie asked Annette that night. The boy had spoken to no one all evening.

"You know Kevin," Annette told her. "He gets moods."

There was no use worrying Sophie who had given them this trip.

13   *The Little People*

Once again Kevin became perverse and uncoopera-
tive. John had saved him from injury, perhaps even
from death, but from that time forward he took a dim
view of the whole trip. Sam had given everyone camp
tasks, but with an ironic little smile hovering about his
mouth, Kevin would start his, then wander away.
Although Sophie was inclined to ignore the whole thing,
Sam became indignant.

Ronnie precipitated the next incident. "Kev! Help
me with these bedrolls."

His brother, stretched beside the dying fire, yawned luxuriously. "Why work when somebody else is paid for it?"

Sophie wheeled on him. "Young man, your father isn't paying for this part of your vacation. Behave and do your share."

Kevin got to his feet and helped stack all the bedrolls, but an hour later Sophie looked about. "Where's Kevin?"

"Said he was going for a walk," Ronnie reported.

Sam frowned. "I said nobody was to go off alone."

"He'll be back." John's tone indicated this was regrettable.

Sophie, however, was alarmed. "You have to remember I am responsible for everyone's safety. If anything should happen. . . ."

Everyone knew she was right. John got to his feet. "I'll look for him, bring him in if I have to drag him." There was relish in his remark.

Sophie gave everyone a direction. "Annette, you and Mary know the Medicine Mountain region. Go hunt there. Ronnie and I will go down the pass."

The girls wasted no time on the mountaintop, which could be seen from everywhere, but went around the base and in an hour found themselves on the west side facing impenetrable brush ahead. Mary looked at the hollowed wind holes above. "Kev's not around here. Let's climb up through those holes and go back to camp over the top. I'm not scared of the little people."

By the time they had covered half the five hundred feet to the top they were slipping from one hole into the next. "Listen!" Annette said suddenly.

Both knew they were listening to the same sound they had previously heard from above. Now located below the sound, it came down to them as a thin disembodied wail that made the skin crawl, made them wonder if any human conclusion could be correct.

Mary shuddered. "I was wrong. I am scared! Let's get out of here." She looked down when they finally reached the top. "If there are little people I don't know where they hide."

At midafternoon John and Kevin were still gone, and Ronnie burst into sudden tears. The girls took him for a walk to ease his worry.

At sundown John walked wearily into camp. "I never saw him all day!"

There was a sound behind them, and everyone whirled to see Kevin, dirty and disheveled, coming down along the rocks. "Look what I found!" He was holding out a small rifle.

Sam's eyes snapped. "Why, that's the gun somebody swiped from line camp. Sophie, that's your initials on the stock."

Sophie moved to him, her hand out. "Let me see, Kevin."

Kevin almost leaped back. "I found it! It's mine!"

Sophie's lips tightened. "I just want to see it, Kevin. Where'd you find it?"

Kevin pointed back toward the northwest. "In a deserted camp over beyond the pass. There was an old blanket, some old bread and bacon wrappers, and this gun hidden under the blanket."

Sophie slipped out the cartridge clip. "Three shells. Now why would somebody go off and leave a good gun in a deserted camp?"

She handed the gun to Sam and Kevin's hands reached in dismay. Sam turned away with it. "This ain't yours, boy. It's Sophie's."

The expressions that crossed Kevin's face were frightening. His mouth opened as though to scream defiance and insults at Sam. He clenched his fists, and Annette realized that this boy was close to violence.

Mary briefly settled the matter. "Oh, come on, Kevin! We've been waiting for you and everybody's hungry." She turned to the kettle sitting close to the fire and dished him up a plate of the rich savory stew Sam had made.

Kevin took the plate sulkily and began eating, but repeatedly his glance flicked the rifle protruding from the pack beside the door of the men's tent.

Supper was a silent meal. John was obviously tired, and the others sensed that things were going badly. As soon as they finished eating, everyone but Kevin pitched in to do the cleanup and to ready the tents for the night.

Annette was on her hands and knees laying out her bedroll inside the women's tent when she heard the sound of a shot outside. She and Mary collided as they rushed outside, hearing the frightened snorting of horses, the pounding of hobbled hooves from the meadow below camp. Kevin was standing beside the fire with the rifle in his hands, looking down at it admiringly.

"Sure shoots nice," he said quietly.

For once Sam was too outraged to bawl at anyone. Instead he spoke through set teeth. "Kid, did you hear those horses?"

Kevin looked at him, frowning in a puzzled way. "Horses? No."

Sam went on relentlessly. "You hear those hooves— off in the distance and getting farther? If I don't miss my guess, you've stampeded the horses, and that means that if White-Eye broke his picket rope, we're going to have one dickens of a time rounding 'em up. We may end up walkin' home! What did you think you were doin' with that rifle anyhow?"

Kevin stared through the darkness from which the plunging sound of hobbled hooves was receding. "I just wanted to see how this worked. I didn't know it would scare the horses."

Sam, beyond speech, gave him a baleful look and disappeared into the darkness with John.

Sophie sighed. "Honestly, Kevin!"

He laid the rifle back in the pack. "Sorry," he said indifferently and entered the men's tent.

Sam and John returned. "White-Eye yanked his pin. From the sound they've gone down the pass. Maybe they'll stop in that meadow beyond, and we can get 'em in the morning."

Sam's daybreak explosion of wrath brought them sitting up in their sleeping bags. Sophie struggled out and began pulling on her clothes. The girls dressed hastily and saw Sam holding Kevin in front of the tent and shaking him. "Where is it? What'd you do with it?"

Kevin had been jarred awake too fast. "Wha—with what?"

His blinking gaze saw the women and he hastily wrapped himself in a blanket which had been dragged out of the tent with him. Sam shook him again. "You know what! The rifle!"

Awake now, Kevin answered Sam's verbal attack with one of his own. "It's in the pack—where I put it last night. Let go of me!" He gave a jerk so hard it broke Sam's hold.

Sophie spoke. "What's happened, Sam?"

"I went to get the bacon out of the pack and the rifle's gone. He's hid it out somewhere."

Sophie went to rummage in the pack. She straightened slowly. "The gun's gone, yes. But so's that other package of bacon and one of the three loaves of bread that were left. Kevin wouldn't take those."

"Sophie, I didn't take any of it!" Kevin said. "I didn't even wake up all night."

Dawn was breaking and by dim light Annette could see his brown eyes smoldering. She saw something else. He was not lying. Sophie saw it, too.

She turned to Sam. "Something else has happened here, Sam. Last night I thought I heard something outside, but when I got up to look out the tent flap, I knocked a flashlight off the pannier. When I found it I had a look but no one was around, so I just went back to bed. I think we had a visitor."

At the startled looks of the girls she tried to lighten the whole situation. "A bear maybe. Bears like bacon."

Sam stared as though he doubted her sanity. "A bear —with a rifle?"

Everybody laughed except Kevin. Sam wheeled on him defensively as though he had to be angry with somebody whether his statement applied or not. "It's one thing to go poppin' a gun off at anything you see. It's another to have both aim and judgment. I doubt you got either one!"

Unexpectedly Ronnie came to Kevin's defense. "He can shoot—whether you think so or not. Last year he won the prone shooting contest at Jefferson High."

"If he's so good, he'd better learn not to stampede horses," Sam snapped back. "Get started everybody. We got to round up them nags today."

They ate a hurried breakfast, and then Sam gave directions. "When we get where we can see down the pass, we'll spread out and try to bunch 'em. If White-Eye's still draggin' his picket rope, maybe we can pick him up, and the rest will come back with him."

"But, Sam," Sophie protested. "Your leg will bother you too much. . . ."

"I know," Sam told her bitterly. "Limpy Leg Sam! That's me! But I'll trudge up to the head of the pass an' wait there to head 'em down into the meadow here if they come runnin'."

At the head of the pass Sam sent everyone on ahead except the girls. "If I remember, that meadow slopes to a dry wash down under the brow of Medicine Mountain. Those nags might get out there, but nowhere else. Maybe you two better climb up over the pass here and cut across to head 'em back if they try it."

When the girls had climbed to the top of the long sloping rock wall of the pass, they could see down into the meadow. John tried to pick up White-Eye's dragging rope and the horse let his hand reach down, then bolted. The others went plunging after him despite their fettered legs. Annette had not realized that a hobbled horse could actually cover ground rather rapidly if he chose to. The valley, moreover, was longer than she had remembered it to be. The band traveled at least a mile before wheeling to look back at their pursuers. Their snorts rang on the early morning air. Cindy had broken her hobbles and she kicked up her heels and raced in circles, exciting White-Eye to even greater rebellion, as the group tried to move up again.

Mary turned to Annette. "Those critters are going to make a game out of this. We'd better get down to the south end. I'll go out in the valley and try to head them back first, but you go down the side of the ridge and get into that wash—fast. One person can turn them there if they get around me."

The girls separated, with Mary angling out into the narrow meadow a quarter of a mile before it narrowed into the wash, and with Annette cutting down the side of the ridge that joined Medicine Mountain on the north. She was almost halfway to the wash when she heard the sound of hooves, looked over her shoulder to see Mary wildly waving her arms at the horses coming down the park toward her.

"Hurry!" Mary shouted. "Hurry!"

Annette ran in under a group of trees, raced around their low limbs and found herself still behind trees on a ledge six feet above the ground. She grabbed a tree limb and leaped off letting the limb carry her down. She lit sliding and sat down, got to her feet hurriedly and stopped.

Facing her, rifle in hand, was Tom Nally.

For a moment Annette felt paralyzed. He was six feet from her, level-eyed and unmoving. He was also unsurprised. His thin lips widened into a chilled amused smile as she stood still gasping for breath from her run.

"Not a word out of you! Keep quiet and come here."

She could not move, but her brain was taking things in. He was deeply tanned now instead of sunburned red. His clothing was in bad shape. The knee of his cotton trousers was ripped, and his blue work shirt had a split up the sleeve and was weathered a gray-white.

Fifty yards below she heard Mary shouting, heard the

pound of hooves as the horses turned back and went clumping up the valley again.

Then Mary was walking toward the timber which hid Annette and Nally. "Annette! Where are you?"

"I said come here!" Nally hissed at her.

Annette started slowly toward him, little shivers running up and down her spine. Without thinking about it, her mouth opened to call to Mary, to tell her to run, but before she could utter a sound, he caught her arm and clapped a hand over her mouth, the rifle sliding down to his feet.

"Now get this straight," he whispered. "You do exactly what I tell you. No more, no less. I want her up here."

Mary was at the foot of the rise to the trees now, looking up at the thick boughs. "Annette! Answer me. Where did you go?"

"Go on now. Tell her to come up here," Nally gritted.

All the things Mary had told her about this brother flashed through Annette's mind. "I won't do it!" she told him. She pulled away, her mouth opening to call down a warning, but the sound ended in a cry of pain.

Nally caught her arm behind her back, pushed up. "I said call her!"

Annette tried to resist. He pushed harder and she cried out again. Then Mary was climbing up through the trees. "Annette! What's wrong?"

Then Mary pushed through the screen of boughs and

came face to face with them. Her surprise changed to fury as she saw Annette bent double trying to get away from the dreadful pain. "What are you doing to her? Let go or I'll scream!"

"No, you won't," he told her. He reached down and lifted the rifle as he pushed Annette over against the wall of the ledge. "Make a sound and I'll use this—on you or anybody else who comes. Stand over there beside her, and listen. I've got an errand for one of you."

Annette was leaning back against the rock holding her arm, and Mary's hands, tense and shaking, took hold of it, rubbing the upper muscles where the strain had been almost intolerable. "What do you want?"

Nally put his foot on a rock, leaned his elbow on his knee, and studied them with grim amusement. "I need a lot of things you've got over there in that camp, sis. You didn't give me any help the last time I saw you. You even threatened to call the police. Now I'm going to get it—from one of you.

"Not only did you not give me a hand when I asked you, but you come up to my hiding place on—of all things—a pleasure camping trip with the works. Two packhorses with equipment, sleeping bags, food, a set of people who have everything. Nice going, sis! I had my last meal of stuff from home three days ago, and I've not dared shoot anything for fear I might need my ammunition more later on."

He saw Annette's eyes drop to the rifle, take in the initials, S.L., on the barrel. "I didn't know you were around until I came back yesterday and found my gun gone. Then last night I heard that rifle crack. I'd know it anywhere. So I had to go steal it back. Reckless, yes. But at least I had bacon for breakfast this morning."

Annette stole a look at Mary. Her chin was high, her lips tight with tension. "Come on," she told him sharply. "What are you getting at, Tom?"

Nally's grin faded in exchange for the expression Annette had already seen too often, a narrow-eyed, cold threat. "Just this. Your friends are still chasing horses, but over this ridge your camp is just a quarter of a mile away." He stabbed a finger at Annette. "You're to go— fast—and get me a bedroll, whatever food you can bring, and some clothes. I saw that big Indian kid this morning. He's about my size. Bring me some of his pants, shirt, coat—shoes, too. You've got half an hour. If you're not back by then"—he surveyed his sister—"just don't forget I owe this girl a few scores and it'll be a good time to repay 'em. Just dandy. She won't be around when you get back!"

He let the facts soak in for a second. Then his voice whiplashed her. "Get going. There's nobody there. I looked just before I came down to cut you off. Get what I need and get back here fast."

"And if I do—what about Mary?" Annette asked. "You'll let her go?"

"If she behaves and you do as you're told. . . ." He left the sentence unfinished. Even as she listened Annette realized it was not a promise.

Mary pushed her away. "Go on, Annette. It's all you can do."

As Annette found a low spot and climbed up over the ledge, their eyes met with the bitter knowledge that nothing this boy said really meant anything.

By the time she reached camp, winded and gasping, she knew she could not bring the others in on this. It would only mean the death of Mary. All she could do was take back what he wanted and hope that he would release her.

With shaking hands she burrowed into the food pack, pulled out the small canned ham Sophie had been saving for the last day, a loaf of bread, part of a carton of eggs, a box of raisins, a box of pancake mix. She snatched up a blanket nobody had used, spread it on the ground and piled the food on it, then rushed into the men's tent to get a bedroll and any of John's clothes she could find.

The men had tossed their used clothing into a pile at the back of the tent. She knelt and began throwing garments aside trying to find something of John's, trying to remember what he had been wearing earlier in the week. The sneakers he wore around the fire evenings were lying beside the pile and she tossed them through the door of the tent and threw a bedroll out after them. Then she reached for a plaid shirt of his that she remembered and the largest of the blue jeans.

It seemed as though time was spinning past her. She got to her feet, picked up John's denim jacket lying across a bedroll, then suddenly froze in her tracks at a sound outside. The tent flap pulled back and there stood John in the door of the tent.

Despite the seriousness of the situation Annette could not help being conscious of how she must look standing there with the Indian boy's dirty laundry in her arms, in the men's tent, where she had no business being. The worst of it was that she didn't dare take time to explain it.

For the first time since she had known him, she saw John caught by such complete surprise that it showed all over him. He had caught her in an act that was ridiculous, suspicious, at least in questionable taste. He could not know that at this moment it was also desperate. If she told him he would interfere and that would be the death of Mary Nally.

14   *Caught in the Act*

Annette tried to carry the matter off on a light note. "Well, you got back early. I needed some things."

Acting as if this were a perfectly normal act, she pushed past him, dropped the clothing on top of the food, and gathered up the four ends of the blanket. John watched, his face so astonished that at any other time she would have laughed. Now she just hoped that he stayed astonished long enough to give her a chance to get away.

She had no such luck. He walked up to stand looking

down at her. "Where are you going with my clothes? And all that stuff?"

Maybe the best way was to quarrel with him, make him so mad he would tramp off and let her alone. "It's none of your business! Maybe I'm going to do the laundry before we go home."

"Just my laundry? Plus a canned ham, a loaf of bread, and a bedroll? You aren't *that* crazy!" Then his hard hand lifted her to her feet. "Where are you going with that stuff? Where's Mary?"

She could think of no more excuses. Suddenly she burst into a flood of tears. Although she wept because she could not help it, behind the tears was the hope that maybe tears were the last thing on earth John could tolerate and that he might be disgusted enough to go away.

Again she had no luck. Instead, he pushed her down on the end of a log and turned her to face him. "Something's happened. Come on, Annette! Tell me! Kevin's on his way back now. Don't let *that* one in on any secrets or he'll ruin everything."

"If I tell you, you'll do something about it and he'll kill Mary!" she sobbed.

His voice suddenly tense and demanding, he stood up. "*Who'll* kill Mary? Hurry *up!*"

She told him because she had no choice. "If I get back in time maybe he'll—*not*—kill her."

She was trying to break his grip on her arm as Kevin walked into camp. "What are you doing to her?"

John still held her arm. "Keep your shirt on, Kevin! Tom Nally's got Mary a prisoner over on the other side of the ridge until Annette brings him supplies. He'll kill her if she isn't back in thirty minutes. Nally means business."

"Who's Nally?" Kevin asked.

For the first time Annette realized that they had all kept Mary's secret well. "He's Mary's brother. He's an escaped convict."

Afterward she was to remember that the faces of both boys seemed to change—John's lost its moody angriness and Kevin's changed from ironic ill humor to stark fear and fury. Both were calculating the odds.

John released her. "Go on back. We'll get you out somehow. I don't know how, but we will. Hold him off. Give us all the time you can."

Annette gathered the corners of the blanket and turned toward the ridge. "He's in those trees, and don't forget he's got the rifle. I saw it." Then she left to face a situation more terrifying than anything she had ever known.

The bundle was not heavy, but it was awkward and things kept trying to slip out through the open sides of the blanket. Twice she had to stop and regather the ends, each time hoping the thirty minutes was not yet up. She reached the top of the ridge and glanced back. No one was in sight.

She reached the ledge below which Nally and Mary were to wait. A sick feeling struck her stomach like a

blow as she saw no one there. Then a low voice fifty
feet to the left along the ridge pulled her in that direction and she saw Tom holding Mary in front of him
like a shield, the rifle pointing at Annette from under
Mary's right arm while he held her left above the elbow
with a grip that cut into the flesh. Mary was biting her
lip to keep from crying out with pain.

"This way," he said, nodding backward with his head.
"Just in case you saw somebody and blabbed, we'll
move."

As she passed the two Annette thought of suddenly
hurling the bundle she carried in his face. Maybe it
would knock the rifle aside and give them time to get
away. He held his sister firmly in front of him, however,
and the ruse would merely hit Mary and not hurt him.

There was no longer the sound of shouts from the
north end of the meadow, no longer any pounding
hooves. Apparently the group had managed to head the
horses back into the pass toward camp. Somehow the
absence of sound dismayed Annette completely, making
her feel that she and Mary were completely alone, and
also feeling more certain by the second that Tom Nally
was going to take them somewhere out of earshot
and. . . . Somehow she could go no farther than that.

Because there was no one in the meadow to see them,
Nally ordered them down into the pasture, then walked
them south for almost half a mile. Annette felt thank-
ful, for the walk took time and time was what John had
said he needed. At this point, what he could do with

time—or anything else—was more than she could understand.

They came to the draw and dropped down into it. The end of the blanket slipped from Annette's grip and spilled the supplies in the brush. She glanced at Nally in dismay.

"Leave it. Start climbing—up the wall there."

Annette looked up. They were under the brow of Medicine Mountain, directly under the catacomb formations in which they had played. There would be no means of escape once they reached the top, for they could be observed anywhere from the top of the peak. Ahead of them in the draw was an almost impenetrable mass of brush and rock.

"He doesn't know this place. He hasn't been here except on the other side of the ridge where John and I left him after the bus ride," she told herself.

Annette, in the lead, began climbing from one outcropping of rock to another with Mary following close behind her and with Nally staying a cautious four or five yards behind them, the rifle ready in his hand. The formations were about fifty feet above them on the steep slope. She tried to swallow her terror as she realized this was where Nally was probably going to finish what he had started.

Then she rounded a rock and came to a shale slide perhaps ten feet long, five or six feet wide. It made her recall John's rescuing Kevin from disaster, made her wonder if she could create such a disaster for Tom Nally.

Deliberately she stepped out on it instead of going around, let her feet scramble for balance, and fell forward clawing at the loose stuff as it began to slide, hoping that Mary could get out of the way in time.

Mary fell but she rolled aside before it caught her. Nally had more time and as the slide deepened and quickened, he leaped clear. He jumped catlike up beside Annette, the rifle clutched as though to strike her. "Don't try that again!"

She went crawling on up, fingernails tearing at the dirt places that wanted to give under her weight, knowing that whatever they did had to be done before he trapped them back in one of the holes.

She was at the entrance to the first when she had a plan, and she wheeled and literally flung herself at him as Mary moved a little to one side. Even coming down at him from above, he had too much weight and bulk for her light frame. He thrust the rifle sideways against her head as she fell, and she knew blinding light for a second, then darkness.

15   *The Prisoner*

She came to as he was pulling her into the first of the holes by one arm. The light filtering down from above came and went momentarily as she stared up, conscious of Mary kneeling beside her, of Nally at her feet.

"Thought you'd knock me off the edge, didn't you? Or make me fire this so somebody'd come for help." He patted the rifle lightly.

Annette's brain was clearing now and so were her ears. From above came the faint *woo—wo—oo* sound of the wind with that peculiarly human cry on its crest.

"What's that?" Nally snapped. "Who did that?" He stepped back, eyeing them suspiciously.

"We didn't. . ." Mary began.

Annette groped for Mary's hand as though she were dreadfully afraid. "It's—it's the little—the little people!" she exclaimed, staring about everywhere except up. Time was what John needed. If she could buy only a few minutes!

"The little people? Don't kid me!" Nally sneered.

Her clearing vision showed him glancing nervously about just as the sound came again, increased but not quite as she had heard it before. This had a different timbre, an eerie howling quality that came at them from the very walls, but not from above.

Something else came from above as Nally stepped fearfully back. Then a filter of dust sifted into her eyes. She shut them and turned toward Mary with a terrified sob. "Don't—don't let them—don't let the little people —" Just before the dust had dribbled down she had seen something move up in the holes, something in the shadows that slipped lower, but to the west side and out of Nally's range.

Then Mary's voice cried out. "No, Tom! Don't do that! They'll catch you! They'll know who did it!"

Annette opened her eyes to see Nally with the gun held overhead as he advanced on his sister to club her down. "I'm getting out!" he gritted. "There's something here. But not before I keep you from talking."

The low-toned howl sounded, and with a desperate

motion he swung the gun butt just as something leaped down on him from above, knocking the rifle from his hand, hitting his shoulder and knocking him flat. The collision knocked John flat, too, his head striking the wall. Momentarily he lay still and Nally scrambled for the rifle which had fallen near the cliff edge. Before he reached it Kevin's head popped up over the edge from below and his hand snatched the weapon. Nally leaped for him. Kevin dodged and Nally fell over the edge and out of sight.

The girls rushed to see and John staggered along behind them. They saw Nally roll to the bottom of the gulch, leap up, and start running down the meadow. Calmly Kevin steadied his footing, took careful aim and fired. Nally staggered, ran again, then fell.

The four of them went sliding down and rushed to him as he made another effort to escape. Something was wrong with his leg, and he whirled on them like an animal at bay. The snarl on his face made Annette want to run.

John whipped off his belt. "Put your hands behind you!"

Nally glared at him, but Kevin took careful aim. Slowly the convict rolled face down and let John loop the belt over his wrist, but when John pulled one foot up to include it in the loop, Nally began a wild threshing struggle that ended with John lying across his head and shoulders and a girl clinging to each leg. Finally they had him trussed like a turkey.

Kevin's shot had caught him below the knee, and John wrapped his bandanna around the wound. He straightened and looked at Kevin. "You got him in a good place to stop him. You might have killed him."

Kevin frowned. "What do you mean? I hit right where I aimed. In the leg."

They saw that he was perfectly serious. He had known exactly where he was going to hit. It had been as simple as that.

John nodded. "You girls go to camp and have a stretcher of some kind rigged up."

Some things about that long terrible ride down the mountain Annette never forgot. There was the speed with which they broke camp and started home. There was the convict with his hateful expression watching every opportunity to escape, and afterward—but only then—there was grim humor in remembering how once he suddenly pummeled the ribs of Big Ned, the slow Percheron, in an attempt to make him bolt. Ned halted deliberately and swung his heavily maned head around to look at the quarry tied to his back as if to inquire about the rush.

There was humor less grim in remembering that, midway of that fifteen-hour trip, Sophie divided among them the one remaining loaf of bread because they had forgotten to retrieve the food Annette had taken over the ridge. Now nobody could say that he had never experienced hunger.

More clearly than anything else, Annette remembered

Sam's sending the women ahead, once they reached the foothills. Annette remembered slipping from a Cindy so tired her head hung low and then seeing Mary dismount and fold up on the ground—physically exhausted, emotionally drained. With Martha's help they had gotten her to bed, and she had not known, two hours later, when the sheriff and two deputies drove out of the yard with Tom Nally in custody.

After that there were four days left before the Ways' departure, and Annette was conscious that several things had changed since their trip. Several times she saw Kevin and John talking.

"Those two are in a strange position," she mused to Martha. "If John hadn't jumped down and hit him, Nally would probably have shot Kevin when he poked his head over that ledge, and if Kevin hadn't grabbed the gun, Nally would have gotten it and shot John. Each one is living because of the other. They know it, too."

John's attitude toward Annette had changed, too, but she became conscious of that only when, determined to know, she asked him a question. "John, did you make those noises to scare Tom Nally when you climbed down through the holes? Somehow they weren't quite the same as when we heard them that first day we made camp. They were worse!"

For a moment she thought he was not going to reply. Then he gave her a wide friendly smile so open and warm that she almost missed his roundabout answer.

"We Injun kids used to have a lot of fun teasing the

little kids with those weird noises."

The greatest change, however, was in Kevin. He came to the kitchen with the little rifle two days after their trip down the mountain. Nobody had argued about who was to carry the rifle that day, and Kevin, his eyes almost never leaving the prisoner, had kept it ready. Of his ability to use it no one had any doubt.

He placed it on the rack with the shotgun over the door. "I've cleaned and oiled it," he told Sophie.

Sophie promptly took it down. "I'd like you to have this, Kevin."

He had looked from it to her, then had shaken his head. "Thanks, but I'd rather not."

"But why? You like guns."

Suddenly Kevin had gone to sit on the stool beside the fireplace, his face turned away, his voice shaky when he spoke. "I don't think I want much to do with guns anymore. I'm sure glad I knew how to use it when it was needed, but that whole thing was my fault. If I hadn't fired it and spooked the horses, Mary and Annette wouldn't have been cornered—with all that chance of getting killed."

Then, without shame, he had turned a tear-streaked face to them. "I think I'll just leave it up over the rack there."

Mary teased him a little later that day. "The day you leave is my birthday. That's mean!"

The Ways stayed another day to enjoy the towering pink cake Martha baked, and then the Lowery sisters had John drive them all to a movie for a celebration. Throughout the Western picture they talked more than they watched because their own experience over-shadowed anything a movie hero offered. Under the chatter Annette was wondering what she could give Mary for a birthday gift.

"I haven't anything for her. Sophie's present would be driving Mary to Greybull to see her mother tomorrow after the Ways were on the bus for home. Why couldn't I have thought of something nice like that?" she mused, feeling disappointed in herself.

Then she remembered what Mary had said earlier that day. "If Mom can talk, I want to discuss getting a job at Greybull. She won't like it because I'll be alone, but that can't be helped."

Suddenly Annette had a wonderful idea.

The next day Sophie let Mary out at the sanatorium, then drove to the downtown district for some shopping and Annette excused herself for some shopping of her own. Later in the day when they returned for Mary, Annette was without the money she had earned during the summer, but she felt more wealthy than ever before.

"This is my present," she told Mary at the dinner table that night. "Now don't refuse it, because I'm not going to exchange it."

Savoring the moment, Mary slowly opened the brown envelope and pulled out a long slip of heavy printed paper, folded and refolded. She frowned, trying to understand it.

"While you were visiting your mother I long-distanced Uncle Archie," Annette assured her. "He wants you to come. Now don't refuse, please!"

Mary was gasping. "But, Annette, I couldn't go to Hollywood. What would I do?"

"Go to school," Annette told her promptly. "Our high school has a wonderful business course. You could finish in three years. Uncle Archie said that he would help."

Mary's eyes seemed to be getting larger by the moment as though a new horizon was opening, as though something unbelievably wonderful was happening.

"Someday he'd have to let me pay it back. . . . He'll have to. . . ."

"Suit yourself about that," Sophie told her. "You just go."

"All right. I—I just will!"

Then Mary was on her feet and running from the room.

"Let her go," Sophie said. "She doesn't like for people to see her cry."

Annette breathed a sigh of relief that Mary had accepted. "You know, though, I don't know what Uncle Archie's going to say when I tell him I spent my summer's wages on a bus ticket for Mary. I didn't mention that. He probably thinks she's paying for it. He insisted I should learn to handle money."

There were wise smiles on the faces of the Lowery sisters. Annette looked from one to the other. "You knew about that all the time, didn't you?"

Martha nodded. "I don't think your Uncle Archie is going to be one little bit disturbed at what you did with it."